Grimm's

Grimm's Grimmest

Illustrated by
TRACY ARAH DOCKRAY

Introduction by
MARIA TATAR

CHRONICLE BOOKS

SAN FRANCISCO

To my parents, who introduced me to the world of books,
and to everyone who then encouraged me to bring them to life.

T.A.D.

ABOUT THE TEXT

The stories in this volume have been based, for the most part, on the third edition of *Kinder- und Haus-märchen (Nursery and Household Tales)* by Jacob and Wilhelm Grimm, which was published in 1822. *Kinder-und Hausmärchen gesammelt durch die Brüder Grimm,* edited by Heinz Rölleke (Frankfurt a.M.: Deutscher Klassiker Verlag, 1985) has been used as the primary German language source. Our versions of "Rapunzel" and "Allerleirauh" are based on the stories as they appeared in the first German edition of *Nursery and Household Tales,* published in 1812. "The Mother-in-Law" appears only in the first edition, and only as a story fragment; the story included here has been completed by the editor. We would also like to note that in German, the text of "The Willful Child" implies no gender for the subject of the story. Grateful appreciation is due to Maria Tatar for her translations from the first edition and her editorial advice on the text.

Printed in Hong Kong.

AN ARTS COUNSEL BOOK

Edited by Marisa Bulzone
Edited from the German by Stefan Matzig
Book and cover design by Jay Anning/Thumbprint
Original oil paintings photographed by Gregor Halenda

Library of Congress Cataloging-in-Publication Data available.
ISBN 0-8118-1675-3

Distributed in Canada by Raincoast Books
8680 Cambie Street
Vancouver, BC V6P 6M9

10 9 8 7 6 5 4 3 2 1

Chronicle Books
85 Second Street
San Francisco, CA 94105
Web Site: www.chronbooks.com

Contents

List of Color Plates

———◆◆———

She set the boy's head on his neck again and folded the handkerchief round it so that nothing could be seen. Then she sat him on a chair in front of the door and put the apple in his hand.

As they were on their way, the one with the pig's heart did not stay with them at all . . . he tore himself loose and ran wherever the dirt was deepest.

One of them noticed on the little finger of the murdered woman a golden ring, and as he could not draw it off easily, he took an ax and chopped it off.

The King's guards attacked him, but Hans My Hedgehog spurred the rooster, and it flew up over the gates.

The kernel was so large that she could not swallow it, and it remained sticking in her throat.

She promised him a piece of gold if he would nail Falada's head on the gate through which she had to pass morning and evening with her geese.

A second snake crept out of the hole, and when it saw the other lying dead and cut in pieces, it retreated, but soon came again with three green leaves in its mouth.

Then the Prince looked at her foot and saw the blood flowing. And he turned
his horse round and took the false bride home again.

65

He heard something fluttering over his head. It turned out to be three crows,
who flew round and round and at last perched upon the gallows.

75

There in the basin lay her two dear sisters,
miserably murdered and hacked to pieces.

85

And the Devil said, "I will make you rich if you will promise me
what is standing behind your mill."

91

It happened that the King to whom she was betrothed was hunting nearby,
and his dogs came and ran around the tree.

99

He heard a voice, and it seemed so familiar to him that he went toward it,
and when he approached, Rapunzel knew him and fell on his neck and wept.

117

Now, when it was midnight and everyone was asleep,
the nurse saw the door open and the true Queen come in.

123

Out from every hole and corner came black cats with red-hot eyes,
and more and more of them came until he could no longer move.

131

Introduction

Since 1823, when the first English translation of *Nursery and Household Tales* by Jacob and Wilhelm Grimm rolled from the presses, German folktales and fairy tales have enjoyed widespread popularity in the Anglo-American world. There has never been a time since then that these tales were not readily available in English translation. Today adults and children read Grimm in nearly every shape and form: illustrated and annotated, watered down or embellished, faithful to the original German versions or toned down in some way. American readers are bombarded on an annual basis with dozens of translations, adaptations, and retellings of the stories from *Nursery and Household Tales,* most of which are aimed at an audience of children. By contrast, *Grimm's Grimmest* shows us the darker side, making available for an adult audience tales marked by scenes of lurid violence and sensationalized twists and turns of plot. The stuff of nightmares, these stories open a window onto the social and psychological landscape of another culture and challenge us to reflect on our own relationship to that world.

Reading through the 210 stories in the Grimms' *Nursery and Household Tales* can be an eye-opening experience. Even those who know that the Goose Maid's rival is "stripped stark naked and thrown into a barrel that is studded inside with pointed nails," that Rapunzel's suitor is blinded when thorns pierce his eyes, that Snow White's stepmother dances to death in red-hot iron shoes, or that doves peck out the eyes of Cinderella's stepsisters will find themselves taken by surprise when reading the graphic descriptions of incest, murder, mutilation, and cannibalism that fill the pages of these bedtime stories for children. "The Juniper Tree," one of the most widely admired of the tales, recounts the story of a woman who decapitates her stepson, chops up his corpse, and cooks the pieces into a stew that she serves to his father. In "Fowler's Fowl," a wizard drags a girl by the hair to a chopping block, cuts off her head, and deposits her mutilated body parts into a bloody basin. "The Girl Without Hands" tells of a father who cuts off his daughter's hands in order to avoid falling into the devil's power. Allerleirauh, in the tale of that title, takes refuge in the woods to escape the advances of a father who is determined to marry her.

Are these grisly and often macabre turns of plot specific to a single culture or do they reflect timeless, universal aspects of the human psyche? A look at the endings for Cinderella (a tale told in Korea, China, Albania, and Polynesia as well as in Germany) reveals wide variations. While Cinderella always lives happily ever after with the prince, her stepsisters and stepmother meet with fates that display astonishing differences. An Indonesian Cinderella forces her stepsister into a cauldron of boiling water, then has the body cut up, pickled, and sent to the girl's mother as a "salt meat" for her next meal. In a Filipino variant, the stepmother and her daughters are "pulled to pieces by wild horses." Other versions of the story reveal a lighter touch at work. A Tuscan "Cinderella" shows the stepsisters making fools of themselves by wearing so much makeup that they appear disfigured to the guests at the heroine's wedding. Another Italian version, elegant in its simplicity, reveals the jealous girls to be "furious as dogs" when they learn that Cinderella has married a prince.

Not every cultural variant of "Cinderella" has a stake in punishing the stepsisters and their mother. An Armenian Cinderella falls at the feet of her wicked sisters as they are leaving church, weeps copious tears with them, and ends up forgiving them for their duplicitous behavior. Charles Perrault, whose *Tales of Mother Goose* (1697) provided the text on which the Disney film claimed to be based, has perhaps the fullest description of a reconciliation scene. The stepsisters first throw themselves at Cinderella's feet and beg her forgiveness "for all the ill-treatment she had suffered at their hands." Not only does this French Cinderella, who is "as good as she was beautiful," forgive them, she also takes her sisters to live in the palace and loses no time in marrying them to "two gentlemen of high rank about the court."

The similarities across cultures undermine the notion that violent endings for fairy tales are peculiar to the Grimms' collection. At the same time, the stories raise important questions about the cause of such rich diversity and why it is that violence plays any role at all in these tales that we consider bedtime reading for children.

We now know that the stories collected in the nineteenth-century folktale anthologies produced by the Brothers Grimm in Germany, by Alexander Afanasev in Russia, and by Joseph Jacobs in England had their origins in an irreverent peasant culture that arose in conscious opposition to the feudal state's ruling class. By overdoing it in the realm of storytelling, these narrators were able to alleviate—if only temporarily—some of the tedium that marked the daily life of their audience, allowing them to indulge in fantasies of wealth, success, and empowerment. For peasants who sat around the fire on long winter evenings repairing tools, mending clothing, and spinning yarn, it must have been a real relief to find distraction in the bawdy humor, bloodcurdling melodrama, and table-turning pranks of the folktale.

The folktales collected in *Grimm's Grimmest* were designed to keep audiences awake, alert, attentive, and engaged in the intricacies of their plot. In many ways, they can be seen as the ancestors of our urban legends about vanishing hitchhikers and cats accidentally caught in the dryer or as the preliterate equivalents of tabloid tales describing headless bodies found in topless bars. But in many ways, it is the horror film to which the matter and manner of these folktales has most conspicuously migrated. Like horror films, folktales trade in the sensational—breaking taboos and enacting the forbidden with uninhibited energy. The plots of both folktales and horror films, as folklorist and cultural critic Carol Clover has pointed out, are driven by a stock cast of characters, one that often frames the central conflict in terms so emphatically polarized that we appear to be in a clear-cut world of good versus evil. Each genre addresses the desires of sensation seekers, of an audience that has a vested personal and cultural stake in the psychodynamics and sexual politics of its represented world.

Our cultural blindness to the disturbing violence of folk culture becomes glaringly evident when we consider the reverence that has been brought to the folktales collected by the Grimms. Even in 1944, when the Allies were locked in combat with German soldiers, W. H. Auden decreed the Grimms' work to be "among the few indispensable, common-property books upon which Western culture can be founded." "It is hardly too much to say," he added, "that these tales rank next to the Bible in importance." Auden's effort to invest these texts with unassailable moral and spiritual authority would have been applauded by the Grimms. "These stories are suffused with the same purity that makes children appear so marvelous and blessed," Wilhelm Grimm declared in the preface to *Nursery and Household Tales*. As Jacob Grimm had pointed out during his search for a publisher, the main purpose of the proposed volume was not so much to earn royalties as to preserve sacred narrative traditions, salvaging what was left of the priceless national resources still in the hands of the German folk. Those resources would implicitly fund a form of cultural consciousness instrumental in forging national identity at a time of political instability and social unrest.

Yet when faced with the realities of folk culture, the Grimms had no reservations about censoring, revising, and reworking tales so that they would conform with the notion of positive cultural values. The stories that appear in the first edition of the collection were to a great extent sanitized, homogenized, and dressed up by the Grimms, who wanted to create a volume that would meet with popular approval, if not necessarily commercial success. In doing so, however, they were also surprisingly tolerant, allowing all kinds of not-so-innocent episodes to remain in the collection, at least in its first edition.

Despite the brothers' editorial efforts, when the first edition of *Nursery and Household Tales* appeared, it met with a cool reception, in part because of its crude content. One critic noted that the few good tales in the collection were overshadowed by large quantities of "the most pathetic and tasteless material imaginable." A second objected to the unrefined language: a bit of artifice would have gone far toward improving the art of the folk and making the tales more appealing. Another contemporary critic was far less tactful, dismissing the entire collection as "real junk."

Wilhelm Grimm, who took the lead in revising the tales as they moved through six successive editions during the lifetimes of the brothers, fleshed out the texts (to the point where they were often double their original length) and so polished the prose that subsequently no one could complain of its rough-hewn qualities. He also worked hard to clean up the content of the stories, in large part because the Grimms had become aware that the volume had genuine commercial possibilities if the target audience was changed from scholars to children. Wilhelm eliminated all allusions to what he coyly called "certain conditions and relationships."

Foremost among those conditions seems to have been pregnancy. "Rapunzel" had been singled out by critics as particularly inappropriate for children in its original version, and was likely to offend parental sensibilities. In the original, reprinted in this volume, we learn that Rapunzel's daily romps up in the tower with the prince have weighty consequences:

At first Rapunzel was frightened, but soon she came to like the young king so much that she agreed to let him visit every day and to pull him up. The two lived joyfully for a time, and the fairy did not catch on at all until Rapunzel told her one day: "Tell me, Godmother, why my clothes are so tight and why they don't fit me any longer." "Wicked child!" cried the fairy.

In the second edition of *Nursery and Household Tales*, Wilhelm Grimm sacrificed folkloric authenticity for cultural correctness by erasing the fact of Rapunzel's pregnancy and replacing covert sexual passion with explicit conjugal loyalty:

At first Rapunzel was frightened, but soon she came to like the young king so much that she agreed to let him visit every day and to pull him up. The two lived joyfully for a time and loved each other dearly, like man and wife. The enchantress did not catch on at all until Rapunzel told her one day: "Tell me, Godmother, why is it that you are much harder to pull up than the young prince?" "Wicked child," cried the enchantress.

Even as the Grimms sought to remove all traces of bawdy humor in the folktales, they rarely exercised their editorial prerogatives to tone down descriptions of brutal punishments visited on villains or to eliminate the pain and suffering of their victims. Contrary to what one might expect from an effort to revise a volume for children's bedtime reading, violent moments were prolonged or intensified. In the first version of "Cinderella," the stepsisters were actually spared their sight. Only in the second edition did Wilhelm Grimm embellish the text with the vivid account of the dove's revenge and with a clumsy attempt to provide a message justifying the bloody tableau at the tale's end: "And so they were condemned to go blind for the rest of their days because of their wickedness and falsehood."

When the Grimms rewrote the tales for an audience of children, they conformed in part to the disciplinary norms found in nineteenth-century children's literature. Next to the Grimms' tales, the most enduringly popular children's book in German-speaking countries is Dr. Heinrich Hoffmann's *Struwwelpeter* (1845). The verses of *Struwwelpeter* recount storylines that are anything but joyful. "Disobedient Pauline" plays with matches despite the warnings of her two feline companions, who are depicted at the girl's grave, mourning her foolishness as much as her death. "Conrad the Thumbsucker" escapes death but his thumbs are lopped off by a tailor with gigantic shears. In one colorful illustration, blood drips from the mutilated hands, and the final page of the story shows Conrad with both thumbs missing. Then there is the case of "Suppen-

Kaspar," who refuses to touch his soup and wastes away, ending up in the cemetery with a soup tureen marking his grave. While many parents may shake their heads in disbelief as they contemplate the image of the anorectic Kaspar and his gravestone, William J. Bennett seems to have found the story so edifying that he included it in a section entitled "Self-Discipline" in his *Book of Virtues*. "The Story of Augustus, Who Would Not Have Any Soup" is designated by Bennett as a tale "in which we see the inevitable result of not eating enough of the right stuff." Here is the ending that is designed to instill "discipline" in the child-reader: "Look at him, now the fourth day's come; / He scarcely weighs a sugarplum; / He's like a little bit of thread, / And on the fifth day, he was—dead!"

In the context of this pedagogy of fear, it is not surprising to find that the brothers included stories like "The Willful Child" and "Hans My Hedgehog" in their collection. It did not seem to occur to them that illness and death were inappropriate punishments for a "willful" child or that it might be frightening for children to hear about the way in which the child's stubbornness manifests itself even in the grave when its arm pushes through the earth. That the mother ends the tale by beating the child's arm with a rod to make it retract is all the more chilling. For us, despite what William Bennett might believe, it is difficult to imagine reading to a child the description of the fate of one of the two princesses in

"Hans My Hedgehog": "Hans My Hedgehog tore her pretty clothes off and pierced her with his hedgehog's spikes until she was bloodied. 'That is the reward for your falseness,' he said. 'Go your way, I will not have you!' And he chased her home again, where she lived in disgrace for the rest of her days."

Today's professional raconteurs, however, report that children are rarely squeamish when they hear about decapitation or other forms of mutilation. Typical Saturday morning cartoon fare shows that grisly episodes often strike them as hilarious rather than horrifying. Obviously this kind of laughter is as much a release for pent-up anxieties as an expression of delight, but it also indicates that the depiction of physical violence in fairy tales has a special appeal for children, and not only in connection with the punishment of villains. Still, when it comes to descriptions of a hero's trials and tribulations, we are dealing with a somewhat different matter. Here, children, who invariably count themselves among the downtrodden and underprivileged, identify and empathize with the protagonist. The more Hansel and Gretel, Cinderella, and Snow White are victimized by the powers of evil, the more sympathy they elicit and the more captivating their triumphs are for children. Wilhelm Grimm's editing procedures here again succeeded in making *Nursery and Household Tales* more rather than less attractive to young audiences.

In many ways, the brothers' collection (at least in its original form) straddled the line between adult entertainment and children's literature. It appeared in print just when folktales were moving out of barns and spinning rooms and into the nursery. The stories they collected could still be considered a source of entertainment for all age groups: a single tale could offer a sobering lesson for children even as it served as a source of lighthearted entertainment for adults.

Many of the tales in this volume ("The Juniper Tree" and "Hans My Hedgehog" are prime examples) have maintained their positions as part of the standard folkloric repertoire in Germany. In this country, however, they never entered the canon, largely because of their violence, preposterously surreal in the case of the first story, sadistic in the other. Other tales have undergone a process of cultural repression for reasons having less to do with their graphic depiction of violence than with their deviation from what has come to be the fairy-tale norm of a beautiful, passive heroine.

In our culture, the first characters that come to mind when the words *fairy tale* are enunciated are usually Snow White, Cinderella, Sleeping Beauty, Beauty (of "Beauty and the Beast"), and Little Red Riding Hood. These are the canonical heroines, four of whom have been turned into powerful cultural icons by Disney Studios. The first four figures are all implicated in a cult of beauty, passivity, self-sacrifice, and domesticity, and they offer us some interesting insight into the reasons why some folk stories survive and thrive in an official print culture while others fail to make the transition from oral tellings for adults to books for children.

On the one hand, it is far easier to read a story like "Cinderella," which features stepmothers and stepsisters withholding love and affection, than "The Girl Without Hands" and "Allerleirauh," in which fathers sacrifice their daughters to demons or attempt to captivate and capture them with an excess of paternal devotion.

Additionally, there are stories like "The Robber Bridegroom" and "Fowler's Fowl," two stories that also remain virtually unknown in our culture. Both are variants of "Bluebeard," a story popularized by Charles Perrault in his *Tales of Mother Goose*, and both give us heroines in danger, one trapped in the cellar of a robber's house, the other trapped in a bad marriage. Yet the two young women, while fearful, remain unintimidated. Using their courage and their wits (the heroine of "Fowler's Fowl" is described as "smart and clever"), they manage to escape death and to defeat their wicked adversaries.

These two stories are rare in their positioning of the heroines as agents of their own rescue. For this reason, it is interesting that they have both undergone a kind of collective cultural repression in this country and only recently been recuperated by feminist writers. It is telling that contemporary novelists Angela Carter and Margaret Atwood have each turned to "Bluebeard" for narrative inspiration and that a visual artist like Cindy Sherman has created a picture book of "Fitcher's Bird" (published here under the title "Fowler's Fowl").

Fairy tales can be seen as one component of old wives' tales, an oral culture of anecdotes, gossip, family histories, and fantasies. To be sure, old wives' tales were not told exclusively by women, but certain stories—"Beauty and the Beast" is a prime example—were considered the domain of female tellers. In her book *From the Beast to the Blonde,* Marina Warner has made a case for the deep "sympathy between the social category women occupy and fairy tale." As she further notes:

Fairy tales exchange knowledge between an older voice of experience and a younger audience, they present pictures of perils and possibilities that lie ahead, they use terror to set limits on choice and offer consolation to the wronged, they draw social outlines around boys and girls, fathers and mothers, the rich and the poor, the rulers and the ruled, they point out the evildoers and garland the virtuous, they stand up to adversity with dreams of vengeance, power and vindication.

Side by side with conciliatory tales ending with wedded bliss are stories like "The Robber Bridegroom," "Fowler's Fowl," and "The Three Snake Leaves," which focus on marriage as the site of peril, betrayal, and deceit. Stories like these give us the dark side of wedding alliances, a side that was no doubt addressed from every angle as the tellers of old spun their tales along with yarn and flax. These narratives made sense in the context of a cultural setting in which women exchanged stories about the fantasies and the experienced realities of romance, courtship, and marriage. But they are clearly less pertinent to the lives of young children, who are enmeshed in complex family dynamics involving siblings and parents rather than romantic entanglements; these stories have therefore gradually slipped out of our cultural repertoire.

Grimm's Grimmest seeks to restore some of the stories that our adult cultural memory is in danger of losing. Many lack the happy endings we associate with fairy tales and confront us with some of the harder facts of life. "The Mother-in-Law" (which has been reconstructed from a fragmentary narrative for this volume) reminds us that the rivalry between a man's wife and mother cannot always be defused, even if it does not take the deadly turn presented in the Grimms' story. "The Death of the Little Hen" moves relentlessly from one tragedy to the next, reminding

us of the bleak realities of an earlier age in which diseases would move from door to door, women would regularly die in childbirth, or a poor harvest would blight the lives of every person in a village. "The Dog and the Sparrow" shows us the weak getting even with the large and powerful, yet it also points to the harsh cruelties of peasant existence.

By giving us a window into the folk wisdom of an earlier age and revealing the wishes, hopes, fears, disappointments, and frustrations of that time, these stories help us to understand just what is at stake in our own cultural stories. The tales we tell each other and our children not only reflect our own lived experience and our psychic realities, they also shape our lives, enabling us to construct our desires, to cope with our anxieties, and to separate fantasy from reality. In "Grimm's Remembered," Margaret Atwood recalled her experience of reading the "complete" Grimm, in which "every bloodstained axe, wicked witch, and dead horse was right there where the Brothers Grimm had set them down, ready to be discovered by us." She concludes her essay with words that hold true for readers today: "And where else could I have gotten the idea, so early in life, that words can change you?"

MARIA TATAR
Cambridge, 1997

The Juniper Tree

LONG TIME AGO there was a rich man who had a beautiful and pious wife. They loved each other dearly, but had no children, though they wished for them very much. The woman prayed for them day and night, but still they had none.

Now, there was a courtyard in front of their house in which stood a juniper tree, and one day in winter the woman was standing beneath it, paring herself an apple, and while she was paring herself the apple she cut her finger, and the blood fell on the snow.

"Ah," said the woman, and she sighed right heavily and looked at the blood before her and was wistful. "If I had but a child as red as blood and as white as snow!"

And while she thus spoke, she became quite happy in her mind and felt just as if that were going to happen. Then she went into the house, and a month went by and the snow was gone; and two months went by, and then everything was green; and three months, and then all the flowers came out of the earth; and four months, and then all the trees in the wood grew thicker, and the green branches were all closely entwined, and the birds sang until the wood resounded and the blossoms fell from the trees; then the fifth month passed away, and she stood under the juniper tree, which smelled so sweetly that her heart leaped, and she fell on her knees and was beside herself with joy; and when the sixth month was over, the fruit was large and fine, and then she was quite still; in the seventh month, she snatched at the juniper berries and ate them greedily, then she grew sorrowful and sick; when the eight month passed, she called her husband to her, wept, and said, "If I die, then bury me beneath the juniper tree."

Then she was quite comforted and happy until the next month was over. She had a child as red as blood and as white as snow, and when she beheld him she was so delighted that she died.

Her husband buried her beneath the juniper tree, and he began to weep sore; after some time he was more at ease, and though he still wept, he could bear it, and after some time longer he took another wife.

By the second wife he had a daughter named Marlinchen. The child of his first wife, however, was a little son, and he was as red as blood and as white as snow. When the woman looked at her daughter, she was filled with love, but when she looked at the little boy, evil thoughts came into her heart of how she could get all her husband's fortune for her daughter and of how the boy stood in the way.

And so she took great hatred to the little boy, and pushed him from one corner to the other and slapped him here and cuffed him there, until the poor child was in continual terror, for when he came home from school he had no peaceful place.

One day the woman had gone upstairs to her room, and her little daughter followed and said, "Mother, give me an apple."

"Yes, my child," said the woman, and she gave her a fine apple out of a chest that had a great heavy lid with a great sharp iron lock.

"Mother," said the little girl, "is brother not to have one, too?"

This made the woman angry, but to her little daughter she said: "Yes, when he comes home from school." And when she saw from the window that the boy was coming, an evil thought came to her. She snatched at the apple, took it away again from her daughter, and said: "You shall not have one before your brother." And she threw the apple into the chest and shut the lid.

When the little boy came in the door, the woman kindly asked him, "My son, will you have an apple?" while she cast him a nasty look.

"Mother," said the little boy, "how dreadful you look! Yes, give me an apple."

Then she spoke as kindly as before, while holding up the top: "Come here and take one out for yourself." And as the boy was stooping over the opened chest—crash!—she slammed down the lid, so that his head flew off and fell among the red apples.

The woman was overwhelmed with terror and thought, "If I could but make them think that it was not done by me!" So she went to her chest of drawers, took a white handkerchief out of the top drawer, set the boy's head on his neck again, and folded the handkerchief round it so that nothing could be seen. She sat him on a chair in front of the door and put the apple in his hand.

After this Marlinchen came into the kitchen to her mother, who was standing by the fire constantly stirring a pot of hot water. "Mother," said Marlinchen, "Brother is sitting at the door, and he looks quite white, and has an apple in his hand. I asked him to give me the apple, but he did not answer me, and I was quite frightened."

"Go back to him," said the woman, "and if he will not answer you, give him a box on the ear."

So Marlinchen went to the boy and said: "Brother, give me the apple." But he was silent, and she gave him a box on the ear, whereupon his head fell off.

Marlinchen was terrified. She began to cry and ran to her mother and said, "Alas, Mother, I have knocked my brother's head off!" And she cried and screamed, and would not cease.

"Marlinchen," said the woman, "what have you done? But be quiet and let no one know—as it cannot be helped now, we will make him into a pot of stew."

The woman took the little boy and chopped him in pieces, put him into the pot, and made him into stew, but Marlinchen stood by and wept and wept, and all her tears had fallen into the pot and there was no need of any salt.

Then the father came home and sat down to dinner and he asked, "But where is my son?" His wife served up a great dish from the pot of stew, while Marlinchen wept fiercely.

Then the father asked again, "But where is my son?"

"Ah," said his wife, "he has gone across the country to his mother's great uncle; he will stay there a while."

"And what is he going to do there?" the father asked. "He did not even say good-bye to me."

The wife replied, "Oh, he wanted to go, and asked me if he might stay six weeks. He is well taken care of there."

"Ah," said the man, "I feel so unhappy lest all should not be right. He ought to have said good-bye to me." With that he began to eat and said, "Marlinchen, why are you crying? Your brother will certainly come back." Then he said, "Ah, wife, how delicious this food is! Give me some more."

The more he ate, the more he wanted to eat, and he said, "Give me some more; you shall have none of it. It seems to me as if it were all mine." And he ate and ate and threw all the bones under the table, until he finished it all.

But Marlinchen went away to her chest of drawers and pulled her best silk handkerchief from it. She took all the bones from beneath the table, tied them up in the silk, and carried the bundle outside the door, weeping tears of blood. Then she laid them down on the green grass under the juniper tree, and after

flew from the fire, singing magnificently. The bird flew high up in the air, and when it had gone, the juniper tree was just as it had been before, and the handkerchief filled with bones had disappeared. Marlinchen, however, was as gay and happy as if her brother were still alive. She went merrily into the house, sat down to dinner, and ate.

When the bird flew away, it lighted on a goldsmith's house and began to sing—

> "It was my mother who slaughtered me,
> It was my father who ate me,
> But pretty Marlinchen looked for my bones,
> And laid them 'neath the juniper tree.
> Kywitt, kywitt, kywitt,
> Oh what a beautiful bird am I!"

The goldsmith was sitting in his workshop making a golden chain when he heard the bird singing on his roof, and a very beautiful song it seemed to him. He stood up, but as he crossed the threshold he lost one of his slippers. Yet he walked right out into the middle of the street with one shoe and one sock, still wearing his apron, holding the golden chain in one hand and his pincers in the other.

He stood still, looked up at the bird, and said: "Bird, how beautifully you can sing! Sing me that piece again."

"Nay," said the bird, "I'll not sing it twice for nothing! Give me the golden chain, and then I will sing it again for you."

"There," said the goldsmith, "there is the golden chain for you, now sing me that song again."

she had laid them down she suddenly felt light and did not cry anymore. At that the juniper tree began to stir itself, and the branches parted and moved together again, as if someone were rejoicing and clapping his hands.

At the same time a mist seemed to arise from the tree, and in the center of this mist it burned like a fire, and a beautiful bird

Then the bird came and took the golden chain in his right claw, sat in front of the goldsmith, and sang—

> *"It was my mother who slaughtered me,*
> *It was my father who ate me,*
> *But pretty Marlinchen looked for my bones,*
> *And laid them 'neath the juniper tree.*
> *Kywitt, kywitt, kywitt,*
> *Oh what a beautiful bird am I!"*

Then the bird flew away to a shoemaker, lighted on his roof, and sang—

> *"It was my mother who slaughtered me,*
> *It was my father who ate me,*
> *But pretty Marlinchen looked for my bones,*
> *And laid them 'neath the juniper tree.*
> *Kywitt, kywitt, kywitt,*
> *Oh what a beautiful bird am I!"*

The shoemaker heard the song and ran outdoors in his shirtsleeves. He looked up at his roof and was forced to hold his hand before his eyes lest the sun should blind him. "Bird," said he, "how beautifully you can sing!" Then he called in at his door: "Wife, just come outside and look at this bird. He certainly can sing." Then he called his daughter and all of his children, and his apprentices, both young men and maidens alike, and they all came to the street and looked at the bird and saw how beautiful he was, and what fine red and green feathers he had, and how like real gold his neck was, and how the eyes in his head shone like stars.

"Bird," said the shoemaker, "now sing me that song again."

"Nay," said the bird, "I'll not sing it twice for nothing; you must give me something."

"Wife," said the man, "go into the shop; upon the top shelf there stands a pair of red shoes. Bring them here."

Then the wife went and brought the shoes.

"There, bird," said the man, "now sing me that song again."

The bird came and took the shoes in his left claw, flew back on the roof, and sang—

> *"It was my mother who slaughtered me,*
> *It was my father who ate me,*
> *But pretty Marlinchen looked for my bones,*
> *And laid them 'neath the juniper tree.*
> *Kywitt, kywitt, kywitt,*
> *Oh what a beautiful bird am I!"*

And when he had finished his song he flew away with the chain in his right claw and the shoes in his left claw, and he flew until he reached a mill, and the mill went "clip-clap, clip-clap, clip-clap." And in the mill sat twenty miller's men hewing a millstone—and they went "hick-hack, hick-hack, hick-hack." Then the bird went and sat in the linden tree that grew in front of the mill, and sang—

"It was my mother who slaughtered me,"

Then one of them stopped working—

"It was my father who ate me,"

Then two more stopped working and listened to that—

"But pretty Marlinchen looked for my bones,"

Then four more stopped—

"And laid them 'neath"

Now eight only were hewing—

"the juniper tree."

Now only five—

"Kywitt, kywitt, kywitt,"

And now only one—

"Oh what a beautiful bird am I!"

Then the last stopped also and heard the final words. "Bird," said he, "how beautifully you sing! Let me, too, hear that. Sing that once more for me."

"Nay," said the bird, "I'll not sing it twice for nothing. Give me the millstone, and then I will sing it again."

"Yes," said he, "if it belonged to me only, you should have it."

"Yes," said the others, "if he sings again, he shall have it."

Then the bird came down, and the twenty millers all set to work with a beam and raised the stone up—hu-uh uhp, hu-uh uhp, hu-uh uhp. The bird stuck his neck through the hole, put the stone on as if it were a collar, flew onto the tree again, and sang—

"It was my mother who slaughtered me,
It was my father who ate me,
But pretty Marlinchen looked for my bones,
And laid them 'neath the juniper tree.
Kywitt, kywitt, kywitt,
Oh what a beautiful bird am I!"

And when he finished, he spread his wings, and with the chain in his right claw, the shoes in his left, and the millstone round his neck, he flew far away to his father's house.

There in the room sat the father, the mother, and Marlinchen at dinner, and the father said, "How light and happy I feel!"

"Nay," said the mother, "I feel so uneasy, just as if a heavy storm were coming."

Marlinchen, however, sat weeping and weeping.

Then came the bird flying, and as it seated itself on the roof, the father said, "Ah, I feel so truly happy, and the sun is shining so beautifully outside. I feel just as if I were about to see some old friend again."

"Nay," said the woman, as she tore her stays open, "I feel so anxious, my teeth chatter, and I seem to have fire in my veins." But Marlinchen still sat in a corner crying. She held her plate before her eyes and cried until it was quite filled with water.

Then the bird sat on the juniper tree, and sang—

"It was my mother who slaughtered me,"

Then the mother shut her eyes and covered her ears and would not see or hear, but her eyes burned and flashed like lightning, and there was a roaring in her ears like the most violent storm—

"It was my father who ate me,"

"Ah, Mother," said the father, "that is a beautiful bird! He sings so splendidly, and the sun shines so warm, and there is a smell just like cinnamon."

"But pretty Marlinchen looked for my bones,"

Then Marlinchen laid her head on her knees and wept without ceasing, but the father said: "I am going out, I must see the bird quite close."

"Oh, don't go," said his wife, "I feel as if the whole house were shaking and on fire."

But her husband went out and looked at the bird—

"And laid them 'neath the juniper tree.
Kywitt, kywitt, kywitt,
Oh what a beautiful bird am I!"

On this the bird let the golden chain fall, and it fell exactly round the man's neck, so exactly round that it fitted beautifully.

The man went back indoors and said: "Just look at the handsome golden chain the beautiful bird has given me!" But his wife was so terrified that she fell to the floor and the cap fell off her head.

Then sang the bird once more—

"It was my mother who slaughtered me,"

"Would that I were a thousand feet beneath the earth so as not to hear that!" the woman cried.

"It was my father who ate me,"

Then she fell down again as if dead.

"But pretty Marlinchen looked for my bones,"

"Ah," said Marlinchen, "I, too, will go out and see if the bird will give me anything." Then she went out—

"And laid them 'neath the juniper tree."

Then the bird threw the shoes down to her.

"Kywitt, kywitt, kywitt,

Oh what a beautiful bird am I!"

All at once Marlinchen was lighthearted and joyous. She put on the new red shoes and danced and leaped into the house.

"Ah," said she, "I was so sad when I went out and now I am light; that splendid bird has given me a pair of red shoes!"

"Nay!" said her mother, and she sprang to her feet and her hair stood on end like flames of fire, "I feel as if the world were coming to an end! I, too, will go out and see if I feel lighter." As she went out the door—crash!—the bird threw the millstone down on her head and crushed her flat to the ground.

The father and Marlinchen heard that and rushed out to see smoke and flames and fire rising from the spot. When it was over, there stood the little brother, who took his father and Marlinchen by the hand, and all three were happy and went into the house and ate their dinner.

The Three Army Surgeons

HREE ARMY SURGEONS who thought they knew their art perfectly were traveling about the world, and they came to an inn where they wanted to pass the night. The innkeeper asked whence they came and whither they were going.

"We are roaming about the world and practicing our art."

"Show me just once what you can do," said the innkeeper.

The first said he would cut off his hand and put it on again next morning; the second said he would tear out his heart and replace it next morning; the third said he would gouge out his eyes and heal them again next morning.

The surgeons had a salve that joined parts together with which they rubbed themselves, and they always carried it with them in a little bottle Then they cut the hand, heart, and eyes from their bodies as they had said they would, laid them all together on a plate, and gave it to the innkeeper.

The innkeeper gave the plate to a servant girl, who was to set it in the cupboard and take good care of it. The girl, however, had a secret lover who was a soldier. When, therefore, the innkeeper, the three army surgeons, and everyone else in the house were asleep, the soldier came and wanted something to eat.

The girl opened the cupboard and brought him some food, and was so in love, she forgot to shut the cupboard again; she seated herself at the table by her lover, and they chatted away together.

While she sat so contentedly, thinking of no ill luck, the cat came creeping in, found the cupboard open, took the hand and heart and eyes of the three army surgeons, and ran off with them. When the soldier had done eating, and the girl was

26

taking away the things and going to shut the cupboard, she saw that the plate which the innkeeper had given her to take care of was empty.

Then she said in a fright to her lover: "Ah, miserable girl, what shall I do? The hand is gone, the heart and the eyes are gone, too! What will become of me in the morning?"

"Be easy," said he, "I will help you out of your trouble—pass me a knife. There is a thief hanging outside on the gallows. I will cut off his hand. Which hand was it?"

"The right one," she

answered. Then the girl gave him a sharp knife, and he went and cut the poor sinner's right hand off and brought it to her. After this he caught the cat and gouged its eyes out, and now there was nothing but the heart missing.

"Have you not been slaughtering, and are not the dead pigs in the cellar?" asked he.

"Yes," said the girl.

"That's fine," said the soldier, and he went down, fetched a pig's heart, and gave it to the girl.

The girl placed all together on the plate, and put it in the cupboard, and when after this her lover took leave of her, she went quietly to bed.

In the morning when the three army surgeons got up, they told the girl she was to bring them the plate on which the hand, eyes, and heart were lying.

Then she brought it out of the cupboard, and the first fixed the thief's hand on and smeared it with his salve, and it promptly grew to his arm. The second took the cat's eyes and put them in his own head. The third fixed the pig's heart firm in the place where his own had been, and the innkeeper stood by, admired their skill, and said he had never yet seen such a thing as that done, and he would sing their praises and recommend them to everyone. Then they paid their bill and traveled farther.

As they were on their way, the one with the pig's heart did not stay with them at all, but wherever there was a corner he ran to it and rooted about in it with his nose as pigs do. The others wanted to hold him back by the tail of his coat, but that did no good; he tore himself loose and ran wherever the dirt was deepest.

The second also behaved very strangely; he rubbed his eyes and said to the others: "Comrades, what has happened? These are not my eyes! I don't see at all. Will one of you lead me, so that I do not fall?"

Then with difficulty they traveled on until evening, when they reached another inn. They went into the bar together, and there at a table in the corner sat a rich man counting money. The one with the thief's hand walked round about him, made a few jerky movements with his arm, and at last when the stranger turned away, snatched at the pile of money and took a handful from it.

One of them saw this, and said: "Comrade, what are you about? You must not steal—shame on you!"

"Eh," said he, "but what can I do? My hand twitches, and I am forced to snatch things whether I will or not."

After this, the surgeons lay down to sleep, and while they were lying there it was so dark that no one could see his own hand. All at once the one with the cat's eyes awoke, aroused the others, and said: "Brothers, just look up, do you see the white mice running about there?"

The two sat up, but could see nothing. Then said he: "Things are not right with us; we have not got back again what is ours. We must return to the innkeeper; he has deceived us."

So they went back the next morning and told the host they had not received what was their own; that the first had a thief's hand, the second cat's eyes, and the third a pig's heart.

The innkeeper said that the girl must be to blame for that, and was going to call her, but having seen the three coming, she had run out by the back door and not come back.

Then the three said he must give them a great deal of money, or they would set fire to his roof. He gave them what he had, and whatever he could raise, and the three went away with it.

It was enough for the rest of their lives, but they would rather have had their own rightful organs.

The Robber Bridegroom

HERE WAS ONCE a miller who had a beautiful daughter, and when she was grown up, he became anxious that she should be well married and taken care of. So he thought: "If a decent suitor comes and asks for her in marriage, I will give her to him."

Soon after a suitor came forward who seemed very well-to-do, and as the miller knew nothing to complain about him, he promised him his daughter. But the girl did not seem to love him as a bride should love her bridegroom: she had no trust in him. As often as she looked at him or thought about him, she felt a chill in her heart.

One day he said to her, "You are to be my bride, and yet you have never been to see me."

The girl answered: "I do not know where your house is."

Then the bridegroom said: "My house is out there in the dark woods."

She began to make excuses, and said she could not find the way to it, but the bridegroom said: "You must come out to me and pay me a visit next Sunday. I have already invited company, and I will strew ashes on the path through the wood so that you will be sure to find it."

When Sunday came, and the girl was supposed to set out on her way, she became fearful, and without quite knowing why, she filled both pockets full of peas and lentils. There were ashes strewn on the path through the wood, but nevertheless, at each step she cast to the right and left a few peas on the ground. So she went on the whole day until she came to the middle of the darkest wood, where it was the darkest, and there stood a house, not pleasant in her eyes, for it was dark and sinister. She entered, but there was no one there, and it was completely still. Suddenly she heard a voice cry—

"Turn back, turn back, thou pretty bride,
Within this house thou must not abide.
For here do evil things betide."

The girl looked round and perceived that the voice came from a bird who was hanging in a cage by the wall. And again it cried—

"Turn back, turn back, thou pretty bride,
Within this house thou
must not abide.
For here do evil things
betide."

Then the pretty bride went on from one room into another and walked through the whole house, but it was quite empty, with no soul to be found.

At last she reached the cellar, and there sat an ancient woman, who nodded.

"Can you tell me," said the girl, "if my bridegroom lives here?"

"Oh, poor child," answered the old woman, "do you know what has happened to you? You are in a mine of murderers. You thought you were a bride, and soon to be married, but death will be your spouse. Your bridegroom wants to take your life. Look here, I have a great kettle of water to set on, and when once they have you in their power, they will cut you in pieces without mercy, cook you, and eat you, for they are cannibals. Unless I have pity on you, and save you, you are lost!"

Then the old woman hid the bride behind a great cask. "Be still as a mouse," said the old woman, "do not stir or move, or else you are lost. At night when the robbers are asleep, we will escape. I have been waiting a long time for an opportunity to save me from their power."

No sooner was it that the girl had been hidden than the wicked gang entered the house. They dragged another young maid with them; they were drunk and would not listen to her cries and groans. They gave her wine to drink, three glasses full, one of white wine, one of red, and one of yellow, which caused her heart to burst. Then they ripped off her fine clothes, lay her on a table, and then they cut her beautiful body in pieces and strew salt on it.

The poor bride was all the while shaking and trembling behind the cask because she saw what a fate the robbers had intended for her.

One of them noticed on the little finger of the murdered woman a golden ring, and as he could not draw it off easily, he took an ax and chopped it off, but the finger sprang up and fell on the bride's lap. The robber took up a light to look for it, but he could not find it. Then said one of the others: "Have you looked behind the great cask?"

But the old woman cried, "Come and eat, and leave off looking till tomorrow; the finger won't run away."

Then the robbers said the old woman was right, and they left off searching and sat down to eat, and the old woman drugged their wine, so that before long they stretched themselves in the cellar, sleeping and snoring.

When the bride heard that, she came from behind the cask, and had to make her way among the sleepers lying all about the ground, and she felt very much afraid lest she might awaken any of them. But God helped her, and she passed luckily through, and the old woman with her, and they unlocked the door and made all haste to leave that house of murderers.

The wind had carried away the ashes from the path, but the peas and lentils had budded and sprung up, and the moonshine upon them showed the way. They went on through the night till in the morning they reached the mill. Then the girl related to her father all that had happened to her.

When the wedding day came, the friends and neighbors assembled, the miller having invited them, and the bridegroom also appeared. When they were all seated at the table, each one had to tell a story. But the bride sat still and said nothing, until at last the bridegroom said to her: "Now, sweetheart, do you know no story? Tell us something."

She answered: "I will tell you about a dream. I was going alone through a wood,

and I came at last to a house in which there was no living soul, but by the wall was a bird in a cage who cried—

> *'Turn back, turn back, thou pretty bride,*
> *Within this house thou must not abide.*
> *For here do evil things betide.'*

"And then the bird repeated its chorus. Sweetheart, it is only a dream. Then I went through all the rooms, and they were all empty, and it was so dark and sinister. At last I went down into the cellar, and there sat an ancient woman; she nodded her head. I asked her if my bridegroom lived in that house, and she answered, 'Ah, poor child, you have come into a mine of murderers; your bridegroom does live here, but he will kill you and cut you in pieces, and then cook and eat you.' Sweetheart, it is only a dream. But the old woman hid me behind a great cask, and no sooner had she done so than the robbers came home, dragging with them a young maid, and they gave her to drink wine thrice: white, red, and yellow, and because of that her heart burst. Sweetheart, it is only a dream. And they killed her, then they ripped off her fine clothes, and cut her in pieces and strew salt on her. Sweetheart, it is only a dream. And one of the robbers saw a gold ring on the finger of the young woman, and as he could not draw it off easily, he took an ax and chopped it off, but the finger sprang up, and fell on my lap. And here is the finger with the ring!"

At these words she drew it forth and showed it to the company.

The robber bridegroom, who during the story had grown deadly white, sprang up, and wanted to escape, but the guests held him fast and delivered him up to justice. And then he and his whole gang were executed for their evil deeds.

Hans My Hedgehog

⬩⬩⬩

ONG AGO THERE WAS a farmer who had quite enough money and property to live upon, but rich as he was he lacked one piece of fortune: he had no children. Many times when he went to market, the other farmers would laugh at him and question his lack of offspring. At last he flew into a rage, and he came home and exclaimed, "I *will* have a child, even if it should be a hedgehog."

Soon after this speech his wife gave birth to a child that was like a hedgehog above and a boy below, and when his wife saw it she was frightened, and said, "See that you have cursed us!" The farmer replied, "It cannot be helped now. We must have it christened, although it will have no godfather." And the wife said, "We can call it nothing else but Hans My Hedgehog," and when it was christened, the priest said, "With its spikes it can't sleep in a common bed." So a pile of straw was laid behind the stove for Hans My Hedgehog to lie upon. There he stayed for eight years, until his father grew tired of him and wished he would die.

But Hans My Hedgehog did not die, and stayed in the same spot. And one day the farmer was on his way to a fair in a neighboring town. He asked his wife what he should bring home, and she told him "a little piece of meat, some rolls of bread, some things for the housekeeping." Then he went to the maid, who wanted some slippers and a pair of stockings. Lastly he asked Hans My Hedgehog, who replied, "Father, bring me some bagpipes."

When the farmer returned home, he brought his wife the meat and bread, his maid the slippers and stockings, and finally he went behind the oven and gave Hans My Hedgehog the bagpipes. As soon as Hans My Hedgehog had the pipes in hand, he said, "Father, go to the blacksmith and have him shoe the rooster. I will ride it away and never return."

The father was glad to be rid of him and had the rooster shod, and as soon as that was done, Hans My Hedgehog sat upon it and rode away, taking with him pigs and donkeys, which he meant to tend in the forest.

In the forest, Hans My Hedgehog spurred the rooster to the top of the highest tree, and he sat there and tended the pigs and the donkeys for many years until there were lots of pigs and donkeys, and all this time his father knew nothing of him.

While Hans My Hedgehog sat on the treetop he played his bagpipes and made beautiful music. Once a King who had lost his way in the forest came riding past and chanced to hear him. He wondered at the sound and sent his servant to see where it came from. The servant looked about, but saw only a little animal upon a tree; it seemed to be a rooster with a hedgehog on its back that made the music. The King told the servant to ask why it sat there, and if it knew which road led to his kingdom. So Hans My Hedgehog got down from the tree, and said he would show him the way if, in return, the King would write a note that promised to give Hans My Hedgehog whatever first came across the King when he arrived home.

The King thought: "I can easily do that, for Hans My Hedgehog cannot read and I can write what I like." So the King took pen and ink and wrote a note and, that done, Hans My Hedgehog showed him the way, and he got safely home.

But his daughter saw the King arriving from afar and was so overjoyed that she ran to meet and kiss him. The King remembered Hans My Hedgehog and said that he had been forced to promise whatsoever first greeted him when he got home to a very strange animal that sat on a rooster as if it were a horse, and made beautiful music. But then the King said that he had written instead that he should *not* receive it, because Hans My Hedgehog could not read anyway. The Princess was pleased and said he had done well, for she never would have gone away with it.

Hans My Hedgehog, however, looked after his donkeys and pigs, and was always happy and sat on the tree and played his bagpipes. It happened that another King came by with his servants, and he had lost his way as well and did not know his way home because it was a large forest. He also heard the beautiful music and sent his servant to find where it came from. The servant went to the tree, saw the rooster sitting at the top of it, and Hans My Hedgehog atop the rooster, and asked what he was doing up there. "I am keeping my donkeys and my pigs, but how can I help you?" Hans My Hedgehog replied.

The servant explained that they were lost, and could not get back into their own kingdom, and asked if he would not show them the way. So Hans My Hedgehog got down from the tree, and told the aged King that he would show him the way if, in return, the King would write a note that promised to give Hans My Hedgehog whatever first came across the King when he arrived home. The King said: "Yes," and wrote a promise to Hans My Hedgehog that he should have this. That done, Hans My Hedgehog rode before him on the rooster, and pointed out the way, and the King reached his kingdom again safely. When he reached his palace, there was great rejoicing.

This King had an only daughter who was very beautiful; she ran to meet him, threw her arms around his neck, and—delighted to have her old father back again—she kissed him. She also asked where in the world he had been for so long. So the King told her how he had lost his way, and had very nearly not come back at all, but as he was traveling through a great forest, a strange animal that sat on a rooster as if it were a horse and made music had shown him the way home. The King added that in return he had promised whatsoever first greeted him in the royal courtyard, and how that was she herself, and that made the King very sad.

But she promised that, for love of her father, she would willingly go with this Hans My Hedgehog if he arrived to claim her.

Hans My Hedgehog, however, took care of his pigs, and they became more pigs, and then more pigs, until there were so many that the whole forest was filled with pigs. And then Hans My Hedgehog sent word to his father to have every sty in the village emptied, for he was coming with such a great herd of pigs that anyone who could butcher should do so.

His father was troubled at hearing this, for
he thought Hans My Hedgehog had died
long ago. Hans My Hedgehog, however,
seated himself on the rooster, and drove the
pigs before him into the village, and ordered
the slaughter to begin.

Ho!—then there was butchering and hack-
ing that could be heard two hours away! And
when it was done, Hans My Hedgehog said:
"Father, have the rooster shod once more at
the forge, and I will ride away and never
return." The father had the rooster shod
once more, and was pleased that Hans My
Hedgehog would never return again.

Hans My Hedgehog rode away to the first
kingdom, where the King had commanded
that anyone who came riding on a rooster
and carrying bagpipes should be shot at,
stabbed, and butchered so that he might
not enter the castle. When, therefore,
Hans My Hedgehog came riding, the
King's guards attacked him with bayo-
nets, but he spurred the rooster and it
flew up over the gates to the King's window and lighted there.

Hans My Hedgehog demanded that
he be given what was promised, or he
would take both the King's life and that of
his daughter. Then the King begged his
daughter to go away with Hans My Hedgehog in order to save both their lives. So the
Princess dressed herself in white, and her
father gave her a carriage with six horses,

40

magnificent attendants, great gold and treasures. She seated herself in the carriage, and placed Hans My Hedgehog beside her with the rooster and the bagpipes, and when they drove away, the King thought he would never see his daughter again.

But things would turn out differently than he thought, for when they were a short distance from the castle, Hans My Hedgehog tore her pretty clothes off and pierced her with his hedgehog's spikes until she was bloodied. "That is the reward of your falseness," he said. "Go your way, I will not have

you!" And he chased her home again, where she lived in disgrace for the rest of her days.

Hans My Hedgehog, however, rode farther on the rooster, carrying his bagpipes to the land of the second King to whom he had also shown the way. This King had proclaimed that if anyone like Hans My Hedgehog should come, his guards were to present arms, salute him, and give him safe conduct.

When the King's daughter saw Hans My Hedgehog she was horrified, for he really looked very strange. But she could do nothing, for she had given her promise to her father. So Hans My Hedgehog was welcomed by her and seated at the royal table with the Princess by his side.

When the evening came and it was time to go to bed, she was afraid of his spikes, but he told her not to fear, for no harm would come to her. Hans My Hedgehog asked

the old King to place four guards by the door of the chamber, and have them light a great fire. When Hans My Hedgehog was about to get into bed, he would creep out of his hedgehog's skin and leave it lying at the bedside, and the men were to run quickly to it, throw it in the fire, and stay by it until it was consumed.

When the clock struck eleven, Hans entered the chamber, stripped off the hedgehog's skin, and left it lying at the bedside. Then came the guards who fetched it swiftly, and threw it in the fire. When the fire had consumed his hedgehog skin, Hans was saved. He lay on the bed and had the shape of a man, but his skin was charred as if he had been burned. The King sent for his physician, who bathed him with ointments and balms, so that his skin returned to normal and he was a handsome young gentleman. When the King's daughter saw that she was glad, and the next morning they woke up joyfully and were married. Hans received the kingdom from his wife's aged father.

When several years had passed, Hans brought his wife to visit his father, introducing himself as his son. The father declared that he had never had but one, who had been born like a hedgehog with spikes. Then Hans made himself known, and the father rejoiced and returned with his son to his kingdom.

The Willful Child

NCE UPON A TIME there was a child who was willful and would not do what her mother wished. For this reason, God had no pleasure in her, and let her become ill. No doctor could do her any good, and in a short time the child lay on her deathbed.

When she had been lowered into her grave, and the earth was spread over her, all at once her little arm came out again and reached upward. And when they had pushed it back in the ground and spread fresh earth over it, it was all to no purpose, for the arm always came out again.

Then the mother herself was obliged to go to the grave and strike the arm with a rod. When she had done that, the arm was drawn in, and at last the child had rest beneath the ground.

The Death of the Little Hen

• • •

OR SOME TIME the little hen went with the little cock to the nut hill, and they agreed together that whichsoever of them found a kernel of a nut should share it with the other. Then the hen found a large, large nut, but said nothing about it, and intended to eat the kernel herself. The kernel, however, was so large that she could not swallow it, and it remained sticking in her throat, so that she was alarmed lest she should be choked.

Then she cried: "Cock, I entreat you to run as fast as you can and fetch me some water, or I shall choke."

The little cock did run as fast as he could to the well, and said: "Well, you are to give me some water; the little hen is lying on the nut hill, and she has swallowed a large nut and is choking."

The well answered: "First run to the bride and get her to give you some red silk."

The little cock ran to the bride and said: "Bride, you are to give me some red silk; I want to give red silk to the well, the well is to give me some water, I am to take the water to the little hen, who is lying on the nut hill and has swallowed a great nut kernel and is choking with it."

The bride answered: "First run and bring me my veil that has caught on the willow branch."

So the little cock ran to the willow, drew the veil from the branch, and took it to the bride, and the bride gave him some red silk for it, which he took to the well, who gave him some water for it. Then the little cock took the water to the hen, but when he got there the hen had choked in the meantime, and she lay there dead and did not move.

46

Then the cock was so distressed that he cried aloud, and every animal came to lament the little hen; and six mice built a little carriage to carry her to her grave, and when the carriage was ready they harnessed themselves to it, and the cock drove.

On the way, however, they met the fox, who said: "Where are you going, little cock?"

"I am going to bury my little hen."

"May I drive with you?"

"Yes, but seat yourself at the back of the carriage, for in the front my little horses could not drag you."

Then the fox seated himself at the back, and after that, the wolf, the bear, the stag, the lion, and all the beasts of the forest did the same. Then the journey went onward, and they reached a brook.

"How are we to cross over?" asked the little cock.

A straw was lying by the brook, and it said: "I will lay myself straight across, and then you can drive over me."

But when the six mice came to the bridge, the straw slipped and fell into the water, and the six mice also fell in and were drowned.

Then they were again in difficulty, and a coal came and said: "I am large enough, I will lay myself across, and you shall drive over me." So the coal also laid itself across the water, but unhappily just touched it a little bit, at which the coal hissed, was extinguished, and died.

When a stone saw that, it took pity on the little cock, wished to help him, and laid itself over the water. Then the cock drew the carriage himself, but when he got it over and reached the shore with the dead hen, and was about the draw over the others who were sitting behind as well, there were too many of them. The carriage ran back, and they all fell into the water together, and were drowned.

Then the little cock was left alone with the dead hen. He dug a grave for her and laid her in it, and made a mound above it, on which he sat down and fretted until he died, too, and then everything was dead.

The Goose Maid

THERE LIVED ONCE an old Queen whose husband had been dead for many years. She had a beautiful daughter who was promised in marriage to a King's son living beyond the open country. When the wedding drew near, the Queen prepared for her daughter's leaving: she got together furniture and cups and jewels and adornments of gold and silver. She gathered everything proper for the dowry of a royal princess, for she loved her daughter dearly. She gave her also a waiting gentlewoman to serve as escort; and they were each to have a horse to ride for the journey, and the Princess's horse was named Falada, and he could speak.

When the time for parting came, the old mother cut her own fingers so that they bled, and she held beneath them a white cloth, and on it fell three drops of blood. She gave the cloth to her daughter, bidding her take care of it, for "you will need it on the way."

Then they took sad leave of each other, and the Princess put the cloth in her bosom, got on her horse, and set out to go to her bridegroom. After she had ridden an hour she felt very thirsty, and she called to the waiting woman: "Get down, and fill my cup that you carry with water from the brook. I would like to drink."

"Get down yourself," said the waiting woman, "and if you are thirsty, stoop down and drink; I don't want to be your servant."

And the Princess had to get down and drink, and could not have her gold cup. "Oh dear!" said she. And the three drops of blood answered: "If this your mother knew, it would break her heart in two." But the royal bride was humble; she did not complain and mounted the horse.

So they rode on some miles farther; the day was warm, the sun shone hot, and the Princess grew thirsty once more. And when they came to a watercourse, she called once more to the waiting woman, for she had already forgotten her angry words, and said:

"Get down and give me water to drink out of my golden cup."

But the waiting woman spoke still more haughtily and said: "If you want a drink, you may get it yourself; I do not want to be your servant."

So the Princess had to get off her horse to drink, and as she stooped she wept and said, "Oh dear!" And the three drops of blood answered: "If this your mother knew, it would break her heart in two."

And the cloth on which were the three drops of blood fell out of her bosom as she was leaning over the water and floated down the stream, and she never noticed it because she was so scared; not so the waiting woman, who rejoiced because now that she had lost the three drops of blood, the Princess would be weak, and she would have power over the bride.

And when she was going to mount her horse again, the waiting woman said: "Falada belongs to me, and this steed to you!" And the Princess had to give way. Then with harsh words the waiting woman ordered the Princess to take off her royal clothing and put on her plain garments, and then she made her swear under heaven to say nothing of the matter when they came to court. If she had not taken the oath, the Princess would have been killed on the spot. But Falada saw everything and kept it in mind.

The waiting woman then mounted Falada, and the real bride the bad steed, and they journeyed on until they reached the royal castle. There was delight when they arrived and the King's son hastened to meet them, and he lifted the waiting woman from her horse, thinking she was his wife; and then he led her up the stairs, while the real Princess had to remain below. But the old King, who was looking out of the window, saw her halting in the yard, and noticed how gentle, fine, and very beautiful she was, and then he went to the royal chambers and asked the bride who it was that was now standing in the courtyard.

"I brought her with me for company; give the maid something to do, that she may not be standing idle."

But the old King did not have work for her and did not know of any, so he said, "There is a little boy who keeps the geese. She may help him." The boy was called Conrad and the real bride had to help him keep the geese.

Soon after the false bride said to the young Prince: "I ask you for a favor, dearest husband. Send for the knacker, that he may chop the head off the horse I came here upon; he was very troublesome to me on the journey." For she was afraid that the horse might tell how she had behaved to the Princess. And when the order had been given that trusty Falada should die, it came to the real Princess's ears, and she came to the knacker's man secretly and promised him a piece of gold if he would do her a favor and nail Falada's head on the gate through which she had to pass morning and evening with her geese, because she wanted to see him again and again. And the man promised, and he chopped off Falada's head and nailed it fast in the dark and gloomy gateway.

Early next morning, as she and Conrad drove their geese through the gate, she sighed as she went by—

"Oh Falada, dost thou hang there."

And the horse's head answered—

"Alas, young Queen, how ill you fare!
If this your mother knew,
Her heart would break in two."

Then she quietly left the town, and they drove the geese to the open field. And when they came into the meadows she sat down and undid her hair, which was pure gold, and when Conrad saw how it glistened, he wanted to pull out a few hairs for himself. The Princess said—

"Oh wind, blow Conrad's hat away,
Make him run after as it flies,
While I with my golden hair will play,
And twist it up in seemly wise."

Then there came a wind strong enough to blow Conrad's hat far away over the country, and he had to run after it. And by the time

he came back she had put up her hair with combs and pins, and he could not get at any, and he was sulky and would not speak to her.

The next morning, as they passed under the dark and gloomy gateway, the Princess sighed—

"Oh Falada, dost thou hang there."
And Falada answered—
"Alas, young Queen, how ill you fare!
If this your mother knew,
Her heart would break in two."

And when they reached the meadow, the same things happened as before, and after they had got home, Conrad went to the old King and said: "I will tend the geese no longer with that girl." And when the old King asked why, Conrad related all that had happened at the gate and in the meadow.

The old King told him to go to drive the geese the next morning as usual, and he himself went behind the gate and listened how the maiden spoke to Falada's head; and then he followed them into the fields and hid himself. And after a while he saw the girl make her hair all loose, and how it gleamed and shone. Soon she said the verses, and there came a

gust of wind, and away went Conrad's hat and he after it, while the maiden quietly combed and bound up her curls. When the goose girl came back in the evening, the old King sent for her and asked the reason of her doing all this.

"That I must not tell you, nor any person," she answered, "for when I was in danger of my life, I swore an oath under heaven not to reveal it."

The old King would not leave her in peace and said, "If you will not tell it to me, tell it to the iron oven," and he went away. Then she crept into the iron oven and said: "Here I sit forsaken of all the world, and I am a King's daughter. A wicked waiting woman forced me to give up my royal garments and

my place at the bridegroom's side, and I am made a goose girl and have to do mean service. And if this my mother knew, it would break her heart in two."

Now the old King was standing outside by the oven door listening, and he heard all she said, and he called to her and told her to come out of the oven. And he caused royal clothing to be put upon her and it was a miracle how beautiful she was, and he called his son and revealed to him that he had the false bride, for she was really only a waiting woman, and that the true bride was she who had been the goose girl.

The Prince was glad at heart when he saw her beauty and virtue, and a great feast was made ready, and all the people were bidden to it. The bridegroom sat at the table's head, with the true bride on one side and the false bride on the other; and the false one did not recognize the true one because she was blinded by her glittering array.

When they had eaten and drunk and were merry, the old King asked the false bride a riddle: What punishment a person deserved who had behaved in such and such a way to her master, and at the same time related the whole story, and asked what sentence such a person merited.

Then the false bride said: "She deserves no better fate than to be stripped stark naked and thrown in a barrel that is studded inside with pointed nails, and two white horses should be harnessed to it, which will drag her along through one street after another until she is dead."

"It is you," said the old King, "and you have pronounced your own sentence, and thus shall it be done unto you." And when the sentence had been carried out, the Prince married his true bride, and they reigned over the kingdom in peace and happiness.

The Three Snake Leaves

A POOR MAN HAD FALLEN on harsh times and could no longer support his only son. Said the son: "Dear Father, things go so badly with us that I am a burden to you. I would rather go away and see how I can earn my bread." So the father gave him his blessing, and with great sorrow the son took his leave.

At this time, the King of a mighty empire was at war and the youth took service with his army and went out to fight. And when he came before the enemy, there was a battle, and great danger, and it rained shot so that his comrades fell on all sides, and when the leader also was killed, those left were about to take flight, but the youth stepped forth, spoke boldly to them, and cried: "We will not let our Fatherland be ruined!" Then the others followed him, and he pressed on and conquered the enemy. When the King heard that the victory was owed to the youth alone, he raised him above all the others, gave him great treasures, and made him the first in the kingdom.

The King had a daughter who was as beautiful as she was strange. She had made a vow to take no one as her lord and husband who did not promise to let himself be buried alive with her if she died first. "If he loves me with all his heart," said she, "of what use will life be to him afterward?" On her side she would do the same, and if he died first, would go down to the grave with him.

This strange oath had up to this time frightened away all suitors, but the youth became so charmed with her beauty that he cared for nothing and asked her father for her hand. "But do you know what you must promise?" said the King.

"I must be buried with her if I outlive her," he replied, "but my love is so great that I do not mind the danger." Then the King consented, and the wedding was solemnized with great happiness.

They lived now for a while happy and contented with each other, and then it befell that the young Queen was attacked by a severe illness, and no physician could save her. And as she lay there dead, the young King remembered what he had been obliged to promise, and he was horrified at having to lie down alive in the tomb, but there was no escape. The King had placed sentries at all the gates, and it was not possible to avoid his fate. As the day came when the corpse was to be buried, he was taken down with it into the royal vault and then the door was shut and bolted.

Near the coffin stood a table on which were four candles, four loaves of bread, and four bottles of wine, and when this provision came to an end, he would have to die of hunger. And now he sat there full of pain and grief, ate every day only a little piece of bread, drank only a mouthful of wine, and nevertheless saw death daily drawing nearer.

Whilst he thus gazed before him, he saw a snake creep out of a corner of the vault and approach the dead body. And as he thought it came to gnaw at the corpse, he drew his sword and said, "As long as I live, you shall not touch her," and hacked the snake in three pieces.

After a time, a second snake crept out of the hole, and when it saw the other lying dead and cut in pieces, it retreated, but soon came again with three green leaves in its mouth. It took the three pieces of the snake, laid them together, as they fitted, and placed one of the leaves on each wound. Immediately the severed parts joined themselves together, the snake moved and became alive again, and both of them hastened away together.

The leaves were left lying on the ground, and a thought came into the mind of the unhappy man who had been watching all this to know if the wondrous power of the leaves that had brought the snake to life again could not likewise be of service to a human being. So he picked up the leaves and laid one of them on the mouth of his dead wife, and the two others on her eyes. And hardly had he done this than the blood stirred in her veins, rose into her pale face, and colored it again. Then she drew breath, opened her eyes, and said: "Ah, God, where am I?"

"You are with me, dear wife," he answered, and told her how everything had happened, and how he had brought her back again to life. Then he gave her some wine and bread, and when she had regained her strength, he raised her up, and they went to the door and knocked and called so loudly

that the sentries heard it and told the King. The King came down himself and opened the door, and there he found both strong and healthy, and he rejoiced with them that now all sorrow was over.

The young King, however, took the three snake leaves with him, gave them to a servant, and said: "Keep them for me carefully, and carry them constantly about you; who knows in what trouble they may yet be of service to us!"

A change, however, had taken place in his wife: after she had been restored to life, it seemed as if all love for her husband had gone out of her heart. After some time, when he wanted to make a voyage over the sea to visit his old father, and they had gone on board a ship, she forgot the great love and fidelity that he had shown her, and that had been the means of rescuing her from death, and conceived a wicked inclination for the skipper.

When the young King lay there asleep, she called in the skipper and seized the sleeper by the head, and the skipper took him by the feet, and thus they threw him down into the sea. When the shameful deed was done, she said: "Now let us return home and say that he died on the way. I will extol and praise you so to my father that he will marry me to you and make you the heir to his crown."

But the faithful servant had seen all that they did, and he unfastened a little boat from the ship, got into it, sailed after his master, and let the traitors go on their way. He fished up the dead body, and by the help of the three snake leaves that he carried about with him and laid on the eyes and mouth, he fortunately brought the young King back to life.

They both rowed with all their strength day and night, and their little boat sailed so swiftly that they reached the old King before the others. He was astonished when he saw them come alone, and asked what had happened. When he learned the wickedness of his daughter, he said: "I cannot believe that she has behaved so ill, but the truth will soon come to light." He bade both go into a secret chamber and keep themselves hidden from everyone.

Soon afterward the great ship sailed in, and the godless woman appeared before her father with a troubled countenance. He said: "Why do you come back alone? Where is your husband?"

"Ah, dear Father," she replied, "I come home again in great grief; during the voyage, my husband became suddenly ill and died, and if the good skipper had not given me his help, it would have gone ill with me. He was present at his deathbed and can tell you all."

"I will make the dead come alive again," cried the King, and he opened the chamber and bade the two come out. When the woman saw her husband, she was thunderstruck, and fell on her knees and begged for mercy.

The King said: "There is no mercy. He was ready to die with you and restored you to life again, but you have murdered him in his sleep and shall receive the reward that you deserve."

Then she was placed with her accomplice in a ship that had been pierced with holes and sent out to sea, where they soon sank beneath the waves.

Aschenputtel

HERE WAS A RICH MAN whose wife lay sick, and when she felt her end drawing near she called to her only daughter to come to her bed, and said, "Dear child, be pious and good, and God will always take care of you, and I will look down upon you from heaven, and will be with you." And then she closed her eyes and passed away.

The maiden went every day to her mother's grave and wept, and was always pious and good. The snow covered the grave with a white handkerchief, and when the sun took it off again, the man took to himself another wife.

The new wife brought two daughters with her, and they were beautiful and fair in their faces, but at heart they were evil-minded and ugly. And then began very bad times for the poor stepdaughter.

"Is the stupid creature to sit in the same rooms with us?" cried her sisters. "Those who eat bread must earn it. Out with the kitchen maid!" They took away her pretty dresses and put on her an old gray smock and laughed at her and sent her to the kitchen.

There she was obliged to do heavy work—get up before the morning, draw water, make the fires, cook, and wash. Besides all this, the sisters did their utmost to torment her—mocking her, and strewing peas and lentils among the ashes, and setting her to pick them up. In the evenings, when she was quite tired out with her hard day's work, she had no bed to lie on but was obliged to rest next to the hearth among the ashes. And as she always looked dusty and dirty, they named her Aschenputtel.

It happened one day that the father wanted to journey to the fair, and he asked his two stepdaughters what he should bring back for them.

"Fine clothes!" said one.

"Pearls and jewels!" said the other.

"But what will you have, Aschenputtel?" he asked.

"Father, the first twig that strikes against your hat on the way home, that is what you should bring me," she answered.

So he bought for the two stepdaughters fine clothes, pearls, and jewels, and on his way back, as he rode through a green lane, a hazel twig struck against his hat, and he broke it off and carried it home with him. And when he reached home he gave to the stepdaughters what they had wished for, and to Aschenputtel he gave the hazel twig. She thanked him and  went to her mother's grave and planted the twig there, weeping so bitterly that her tears fell upon it and watered it, and it flourished and became a fine tree. Aschenputtel went to see it three times a day, and wept and prayed, and each time, a bird came to the tree, and brought her whatever she had wished for.

Now it came to pass that the King ordained a feast that should last for three days so that the King's son might choose a bride. When the two stepdaughters heard that they were bidden to appear, they felt very pleased, and they called Aschenputtel and said, "Comb our hair, brush our shoes, and make our buckles fast, we are going to the feast at the King's castle."

Aschenputtel did as she was told, but cried, for she, too, would have liked to go to the feast, and she begged her stepmother to allow her to join her stepsisters.

"What, you Aschenputtel?" she exclaimed. "You, who have no dress and no shoes? You, who cannot dance? You want to go to the feast? "

But as she persisted in asking, at last the stepmother said, "I have strewn a dish full of lentils in the ashes, and if you can pick them all up again in two hours, you shall go with us."

Then the maiden went to the back door that led into the garden and called out—

"Oh gentle doves, Oh turtle doves,
And all the birds that be,
The lentils that in ashes lie,
Come and pick up for me!
The good must be put in the dish,
The bad you may eat if you wish."

Then there came to the kitchen window two white doves, and after them the turtle doves, and at last a crowd of all the birds under heaven, chirping and fluttering, and they alighted among the ashes. The doves nodded with their heads and began to pick, peck, pick, peck, and then all the others began to pick, peck, pick, peck, and put all the good grains into the dish. Before an hour was over, all was done, and they flew away. Then the maiden brought the dish to her stepmother, feeling joyful, and thinking that now she should go to the feast, but the stepmother said, "No, Aschenputtel, you have no clothes, and you do not know how to dance, and you are not allowed to come with us!"

And when Aschenputtel cried, she added, "If you can pick two dishes full of lentils out of the ashes, nice and clean, you shall go with us," thinking to herself, "for that is not possible."

Now she strew two dishes full of lentils among the ashes, and the maiden went through the back door into the garden and cried—

> "Oh gentle doves, Oh turtle doves,
> And all the birds that be,
> The lentils that in ashes lie,
> Come and pick up for me!
> The good must be put in the dish,
> The bad you may eat if you wish."

So there came to the kitchen window two white doves, and then the turtle doves, and at last a crowd of all the other birds under heaven, chirping and fluttering, and they alighted among the ashes. The doves nodded with their heads and began to pick, peck, pick, peck, and then all the

others began to pick, peck, pick, peck, and put all the good grains into the dishes. And before a half hour was over, it was all done, and they flew away. Then the maiden took the dishes to the stepmother, feeling joyful, and thinking that now she should go with them to the feast, but she said, "All this is of no good to you. You cannot come with us, for you have no clothes and cannot dance; we would have to be ashamed of you."

Then she set out with her two proud daughters.

And as there was no one left in the house, Aschenputtel went to her mother's grave, sat under the hazel tree, and cried—

"Little tree, little tree, shake over me,
That silver and gold may come down
and cover me."

Then the bird threw down a dress of gold and silver, and a pair of slippers embroidered with silk and silver. And she put on the dress and went to the festival. But her stepmother and sisters did not know her, and thought she must be a foreign princess, she looked so beautiful in her rich dress. Of Aschenputtel they never thought at all and supposed that she was sitting at home in the ashes. The King's son came to meet her and took her by the hand and danced with her. He refused to stand up with anyone else, so that he did not let go her hand, and when anyone came to request it, he answered, "She is my partner."

And when the evening came, she wanted to go home, but the Prince said he would go and accompany her, for he wanted to see who the beautiful maiden belonged to. But she escaped him on the way and jumped up into the pigeon house. Then the Prince waited until her father came and told him the strange maiden had jumped into the pigeon house. The father thought to himself, "Could it be Aschenputtel?" and he called for axes and hatchets and had the pigeon house cut down, but there was no one in it. And when they entered the house, there sat Aschenputtel in her dirty clothes among the ashes, with a little oil lamp burning dimly in the chimney; for Aschenputtel had jumped quickly out of the pigeon house again, and gone to the hazel tree. There she had taken off her beautiful dress and laid it on the grave, and the bird had carried it away again, and then she had put on her little gray smock again and sat down in the kitchen among the ashes.

The next day, when the festival began anew, and the parents and stepsisters had gone to it, Aschenputtel went to the hazel tree and cried—

"Little tree, little tree, shake over me,
That silver and gold may come down
and cover me."

Then the bird cast down a still more splendid dress than on the day before. And when she appeared in it among the guests,

everyone was astonished at her beauty. The Prince had been waiting until she came, and he took her hand and danced only with her. And when anyone else came to invite her, he said, "She is my partner."

And when the evening came, she wanted to go home, and the Prince followed her, for he wanted to see which house she went to, but she escaped from him and ran into the garden at the back of the house. There stood a fine large tree, bearing splendid pears. She leaped as lightly as a squirrel among the branches, and the Prince did not know what had become of her. So he waited until her father came, and then he told him that the strange maiden had rushed from him, and that he thought she had gone up into the pear tree. The father thought to himself, "Could it be Aschenputtel?" and he called for an ax and felled the tree, but there was no one in it. And when they went into the kitchen, there sat Aschenputtel among the ashes as usual, for she had got down the other side of the tree, and had taken back her beautiful clothes to the bird on the hazel tree, and had put on her old gray smock again.

On the third day of the feast, when the parents and the stepdaughters had set off, Aschenputtel went again to her mother's grave and said to the tree—

"Little tree, little tree, shake over me,
That silver and gold may come down
and cover me."

Then the bird cast down a dress, the like of which had never been seen for splendor, and slippers that were of pure gold.

And when she appeared at the feast nobody knew what to say for wonderment. The Prince danced only with her, and if anyone else invited her, he answered, "She is my partner."

And when evening came, Aschenputtel wanted to go home, and the Prince was to accompany her, but she escaped so quickly that he could not follow her. But he had caused all the steps to be spread with pitch, so that the left shoe of the maiden remained sticking in it. The Prince picked it up and saw that it was of pure gold, and very small and slender. The next morning he went to her father and told him that none should be his bride save the one whose foot the golden shoe should fit. Then the two sisters were very glad because they had pretty feet.

The eldest went to her room to try on the shoe, and her mother stood by. But she could not get her great toe into it, for the shoe was too small. Then her mother handed her a knife and said, "Cut the toe off, for when you are queen you will never need to go by foot."

So the girl chopped her toe off, squeezed her foot into the shoe, and went to the Prince. Then he took her with him on his horse as his bride, and with her rode off. But they had to pass by the grave, and there sat

the two white doves in the hazel tree, and
they cried—

>*"That is not the right bride.*
>*The slipper is much too small,*
>*Blood is flowing inside.*
>*It does not fit her at all."*

Then the Prince looked at her foot and
saw the blood flowing. And he turned his
horse round and took the false bride home
again, and said she was not the right one,
and that the other sister must try on the
shoe. So she went into her room and got her
toes in, but her heel was too large. Then
her mother handed her a knife and said,
"Cut a piece off your heel; when you are
queen you will never need to go by foot."
So the girl cut a piece off her heel and
squeezed her foot into the shoe, and went to
the Prince, who took his bride before him
on his horse and rode off. When they
passed by the hazel tree, the two white
doves sat there and cried—

>*"Go back, go back,*
>*There is blood in the shoe.*
>*The shoe is too small,*
>*That bride will not do."*

Then the Prince looked at her foot and saw the blood flowing. And he turned his horse round and brought the false bride home again.

"This is not the right one either," he said. "Have you no other daughter?"

"No," said the man, "only my dead wife left behind her a little nasty Cinderella. It is impossible that she can be the bride." The King's son ordered her to be sent for, but the mother said, "Oh no! She is much too dirty. I could not let her be seen."

But the Prince would have her fetched, and so Aschenputtel had to be called.

Then she washed her face and hands very clean, and then went in and curtseyed to the Prince, who held out to her the golden shoe. Then she drew her left foot out of the heavy shoe she was wearing, and slipped it into the golden one, which fit like a glove. And when she stood up and the Prince looked in her face, he knew again the beautiful maiden that had danced with him, and he cried, "This is the right bride!"

The stepmother and the two sisters were terrified and grew pale with anger, but he put Aschenputtel before him on his horse and rode off. And as they passed the hazel tree, the two white doves cried—

"Coo, Coo,
No blood in her shoe.
She is the right bride,
With the Prince by her side."

And when they had thus cried, they came flying after and perched on Aschenputtel's shoulders, one on the right, the other on the left, and so they remained.

And when her wedding with the Prince was appointed to be held, the false sisters came, hoping to curry favor and to take part in the fortune. As the bride and groom went to the church, the eldest walked on the right side and the younger on the left, and the doves picked out an eye of each of them. And as they returned, the elder was on the left side and the younger on the right, and the doves picked out the other eye of each of them. And so they were condemned to go blind for the rest of their days because of their wickedness and falsehood.

The Crows

A WORTHY SOLDIER had saved a good deal of money from his pay, for he worked hard and did not spend all he earned at the inn, eating and drinking, as all the others did. Now he had two comrades who were rogues and wanted to rob him of his money, but they behaved outwardly toward him in a friendly way. "Listen," said they to him one day, "why should we stay here shut up in this town like prisoners, when you at any rate could live proper and happy at home?" They talked so often to him in this manner that he at last agreed and was willing to run away with them, but they all the time thought of nothing but how they should manage to steal his money from him.

When they had gone a little way, the two rogues said, "We must go by the right-hand road, for that will take us quickest to the border." Now they knew all the while that what they were saying was untrue. As soon as the soldier said, "No, that will take us straight back into the town we came from. We must keep on the left hand," they picked a quarrel with him, and said, "What do you give yourself airs for? You know nothing about it," and then they fell upon him and took his money. But it was not enough until they put out his eyes and dragged him to a gallows that stood hard by, bound him fast, and then they left and went back into the town with the money. But the poor blind man did not know where he was; he felt all around him and, finding that it was below a beam of wood, thought that it was a cross, and said, "After all, they have done kindly in leaving me under a cross; now heaven will guard me." So he raised himself up and began to pray.

As night approached, he heard something fluttering over his head. It turned out to be three crows, who flew round and round and at last perched upon the gallows. By and by, they began to talk together, and he heard one of them say, "Sister, what is the best news with you today?"

"Oh, if men knew what we know!" said the other, "the Princess is ill, and the King has vowed to marry her to anyone who will cure her; but this no one can do, for she will not be well until the toad of this pond is burnt to ashes and the ashes swallowed by the Princess."

"Oh, indeed," said the first crow, "if men did but know what we know! Tonight will fall from heaven a dew of such wonder and healing power that the blind man who washes his eyes with it will see again."

And the third spoke, and said, "Oh, if men knew what we know! The toad is wanted but for one, the dew is wanted but for few. But there is a great dearth of water in the town; all the wells are dried up, and no one knows that they must take the large square stone out of the marketplace and dig underneath it, and that then the finest water will spring up."

When the three crows had done talking, the man heard them fluttering round again, and at last away they <u>flew</u>. Greatly wondering at what he had heard, and overjoyed at the thoughts of getting his sight back, he tried with all his strength to break loose from his bonds. At last he found himself free, and he plucked some of the grass that grew beneath him and washed his eyes with the dew that had fallen upon it. At once his eyesight came to him again, and he saw by the light of the moon and the stars that he was beneath the gallows, and not the cross, as he had thought. Then he gathered together in a bottle as much of the dew as he could to take away with him, and then he went to the pond, dug off the water, fetched the toad and burnt it to ashes. And with the ashes, he set out on his way toward the King's court.

When the soldier reached the palace, he told the King he was come to cure the Princess; and when she had taken of the ashes and been made well, he claimed her for his wife, as the reward that was to be given.

But the King, looking upon him and seeing that his clothes were so shabby, would not keep his word, and said, "Whoever wants to have the Princess for his wife must find water for the town," and thought to get rid of him that way.

But the soldier went out and told the people to take up the square stone in the marketplace and dig for water underneath; and when they had done so there came up a fine spring. So the King could no longer get off giving him his daughter, and they were married and lived happily together.

Some time after, as the man was walking one day through a field, he met his two former comrades who had treated him so basely. Though they did not know him, he knew them at once, and went up to them and said, "Look upon me, I am your old comrade whom you beat and robbed and left blind. Heaven has defeated your wicked wishes and turned all the mischief that you brought upon me into good luck."

When they heard this they fell at his feet and begged for pardon, and because he had a kind and good heart, so he forgave them and took them to his palace and gave them food and clothes. And he told them all that had happened to him, and how he had reached these honors. After they had heard the whole story, they said to themselves, "Why should we not go and sit some night under the gallows? We may hear something that will bring us good luck, too."

The next night they stole away, and when they sat under the gallows a little while, they heard a fluttering noise over their heads, and the three crows came and perched upon it.

"Sisters," said one of them, "someone must have overheard us, for all the world is talking of the wonderful things that have happened: the Princess is well, the toad is taken out of the pond, a blind man's sight has been given him again, and they have dug a fresh well that gives water to the whole town. Let us look about; perhaps we may find someone near. If we do, he shall rue the day."

Then they began to flutter about, found the two men, and flew at them in a rage, beating and pecking them in the face with their wings and beaks till the men were quite blind and lay dead upon the ground under the gallows.

Days passed, and they did not return to the palace. Their old comrade began to wonder where they had been, and he went out in search of them, but he did not find anything but their bones, so he took them from the gallows and buried them in the ground.

Prudent Hans

NE DAY, Hans's mother said, "Where are you going, Hans?"
Hans answered, "To Grethel's, Mother."
"Take care, Hans." "All right! Good-bye, Mother."
"Good-bye, Hans."
Then Hans came to Grethel's. "Good morning, Grethel."
"Good morning, Hans. What have you brought me today?"
"I have brought nothing, but I want something."

So Grethel gave Hans a needle, and then he said, "Good-bye, Grethel," and she said, "Good-bye, Hans." Hans carried the needle away with him and stuck it in a haycart that was going along, and he followed it home.

"Good evening, Mother." "Good evening, Hans. Where have you been?"

"To Grethel's, Mother." "What did you take her?"

"I took nothing, but I brought away something." "What did Grethel give you?"

"A needle, Mother." "What did you do with it, Hans?"

"Stuck it in the haycart." "That was very stupid of you, Hans. You should have stuck it in your sleeve."

"All right, Mother! I'll do better next time."

When next time came, Hans's mother said, "Where are you going, Hans?" "To Grethel's, Mother."

"Take care, Hans."

Then Hans came to Grethel's. "Good morning, Grethel."

"Good morning, Hans. What have you brought me today?"

"I've brought nothing, but I want something."

So Grethel gave Hans a knife, and then he said, "Good-bye, Grethel," and she said, "Good-bye, Hans." Hans took the knife away with him and stuck it in his sleeve, and went home.

"Good evening, Mother." "Good evening, Hans. Where have you been?"

"To Grethel's." "What did you take her?"

"I took nothing, but I brought away something." "What did Grethel give you, Hans?"

"A knife, Mother." "What did you do with it, Hans?"

"Stuck it in my sleeve, Mother."

"That was very stupid of you, Hans. You should have put it in your pocket."

"All right, Mother!" I'll do better next time."

When next time came, Hans's mother said, "Where to, Hans?" "To Grethel's, Mother."

"Take care, Hans."

So Hans came to Grethel's. "Good morning, Grethel."

"Good morning, Hans. What have you brought me today?" "I've brought nothing, but I want to take away something."

So Grethel gave Hans a young goat. "Good-bye, Grethel," he said, and she said, "Good-bye, Hans."

Hans carried off the goat, tied its legs together, and put it in his pocket, and by the time he got home it was suffocated.

"Good evening, Mother."

"Good evening, Hans. Where have you been?"

"To Grethel's, Mother." "What did you take her, Hans?"

"I took nothing, but I brought away something." "What did Grethel give you, Hans?"

"A goat, Mother." "What did you do with it, Hans?"

"Put it in my pocket, Mother." "That was very stupid of you, Hans. You should have tied a cord round its neck and led it home."

"All right, Mother! I'll do better next time."

Then when next time came. "Where to, Hans?" "To Grethel's, Mother."

"Take care, Hans."

Then Hans came to Grethel's. "Good morning, Grethel."

"Good morning, Hans. What have you brought me today?" "I've brought nothing, but I want to take away something."

So Grethel gave Hans a piece of bacon. Then he said, "Good-bye, Grethel." She said, "Good-bye, Hans."

Hans took the bacon, tied a string round it, and dragged it after him on his way home. The dogs came and ate it up, so that when he got home he had the string in his hand and nothing at the other end of it.

"Good evening, Mother." "Good evening, Hans. Where have you been?"

"To Grethel's, Mother." "What did you take her, Hans?"

"I took her nothing, but I brought away something." "What did Grethel give you, Hans?"

"A piece of bacon, Mother." "What did you do with it, Hans?"

"I tied a piece of string to it, and led it home, but the dogs ate it, Mother." "That was very stupid of you, Hans. You ought to have carried it on your head."

"All right! I'll do better next time, Mother."

When the next time came, "Where to, Hans?" "To Grethel's, Mother."

"Take care, Hans."

Then Hans came to Grethel's. "Good morning, Grethel." "Good morning, Hans. What have you brought me?"

"I have brought nothing, but I want to take away something." So Grethel gave Hans a calf. "Good-bye, Grethel." "Good-bye, Hans."

Hans took the calf, set it on his head, and carried it home, and the calf kicked him in his face.

"Good evening, Mother." "Good evening, Hans. Where have you been?"

"To Grethel's, Mother." "What did you take her?"

"I took nothing, but I brought away something." "What did Grethel give you, Hans"

"A calf, Mother." "What did you do with the calf, Hans?"

"I carried it home on my head, but it kicked my face." "That was very stupid of you, Hans. You ought to have led home the calf, and tied it to the manger."

"All right! I'll do better next time, Mother."

When next time came, "Where to, Hans?" "To Grethel's, Mother."

"Take care, Hans."

Then Hans came to Grethel's. "Good morning, Grethel."

"Good morning, Hans. What have you brought me today?" "I have brought nothing, but I want to take away something."

Then Grethel said to Hans, "You shall take away me."

Then Hans took Grethel, tied a rope round her neck, and led her home, fastened her up to the manger, and went to his mother.

"Good evening, Mother." "Good evening, Hans. Where have you been?"

"To Grethel's, Mother." "What did you take her, Hans?"

"Nothing, Mother." "What did Grethel give you, Hans?"

"Nothing but herself, Mother." "Where have you left Grethel, Hans?"

"I led her home with a rope and tied her up to the manger to eat hay, Mother."

"That was very stupid of you, Hans. You should have cast sheep's eyes at her."

"All right, Mother! I'll do better next time."

Then Hans went to the stable, took the eyes from the sheep, and threw them in Grethel's face. Then Grethel became angry, and ran away to become the bride of another.

Fowler's Fowl

IN OLDEN TIMES there was a sorcerer who dressed himself as a pauper and went begging from house to house and stole away pretty girls. No one knew where he took them because none ever came back. One day the sorcerer knocked at the door of a man who had three beautiful daughters. He feigned weakness and carried an old battered basket on his back to hold any gifts he might be offered. He asked for a bite of food and the eldest girl came out to give him a piece of bread. At the sorcerer's touch, she came under his spell and could not help herself from jumping into his basket.

At that, he hurried off with a powerful stride and carried her to his house in the middle of a dark forest. Everything in the house was magnificent and the sorcerer gave the girl whatever she could wish, saying to her, "My darling, you will be happy here with me; you have everything your heart desires."

It went this way for a couple of days and then the sorcerer said, "I must go away on a journey and leave you alone for a while. Here are the keys of the house: you may go anywhere and look at everything, but one room is opened with this little key, and I forbid you to enter it under pain of death." He also gave her an egg and said, "Look after this egg very carefully and carry it wherever you go, because something terrible will happen if it gets lost." She took the keys and the egg and promised to take good care of everything.

When he had gone, the girl went through the house from top to bottom and looked at everything. The rooms glittered with silver and gold and it seemed to her that she had never seen such great splendor. Finally she came to the forbidden door; she meant to walk past, but curiosity nagged at her. She looked at the key; it looked like any ordinary key. She put it in the keyhole and turned it just a little bit, but the door sprang open. And what did she see? A great bloody basin stood in the middle of

the room. It was filled with the parts of dead bodies that had been hacked to pieces; beside it stood a butcher's block with a gleaming ax on top. The girl was so horrified that she dropped the egg, which she held in her hand, and it fell into the basin. She quickly picked it out and wiped off the blood, but her efforts were in vain because the blood reappeared in a moment. She washed and scrubbed, but it would not come clean.

It was not long before the man came back from his journey and the first things he asked for were the key and the egg. She gave them to him but she was trembling, and he could tell from the red spots on the egg that she had been in the bloody chamber. "You have gone in the room against my will," he said. "And shall go back against your own. Your life is finished." He threw her down, dragged her in by the hair, and cut her head off on the block. Then he hacked her to pieces so that the blood flowed all over the floor, and tossed her into the basin with the rest of his victims.

"Now I'll go and get the second one," said the sorcerer, and again he went back to the house disguised as a poor man begging for food. The second daughter brought him a piece of bread and he caught her as he had the first by just touching her and then carried

her away. She fared no better than her sister, for her curiosity led her astray: she opened the door to the bloody chamber, looked inside, and paid with her life.

Now the sorcerer went and fetched the third girl, but she was smart and clever. When he had given her the key and the egg and gone on his journey, she first carefully put the egg away, then she looked all around the house and finally went into the forbidden room. Ah, what she did see! There in the basin lay her two dear sisters, miserably murdered and hacked into pieces. But she got her wits about her and set to work and gathered all the parts and laid them in the right order: head, body, arms, and legs. And when nothing was missing, the limbs began to move and joined together and the two girls opened their eyes and were alive again. They were happy and kissed and hugged one another, and then the third one let her sisters out of the horrible room and hid them away.

When he returned, the sorcerer immediately demanded the key and egg, and as he could see no trace of blood, he said, "You have passed the test and shall be my bride."

"I will marry you," she answered, "but first you must take a basket full of gold to my father and mother, and you must carry it on

your own back. Meanwhile I will get everything ready for the wedding." Then she ran
to where her sisters were hidden and said,
"Now is the time that I can save you. The
wretched man himself shall carry you home,
but send help to me as soon as you arrive."
She put both of them into the basket and covered them with gold so that they could not be
seen. Then she called the sorcerer and said,
"Now take the basket, and don't stop to rest
on the way. I'll be keeping guard from my little window to make sure that you don't."

The sorcerer lifted the basket onto his
shoulders and walked off with it. But it was
so painfully heavy that the sweat streamed
down his face and he feared that he
would be pressed to death. He sat

down to rest awhile, but right away one of
the girls in the basket cried, "I'm looking out
my window and can see you resting! Get up
and go on at once!" He thought it was his
bride calling to him and got up and went on
his way. Again he wanted to sit down, but
right away the voice cried, "I'm looking out
of my window and can see you resting! Get
up and go on at once!" Each time he tried to
stop, the voice would call to him and he had
to keep going until finally, groaning and out
of breath, he brought the basket with the
gold and the two girls into their
parents' house.

At home, meanwhile, the bride was getting everything ready for the wedding and sending out the invitations to the sorcerer's friends. Then she took a skull with its mouth still filled with grinning teeth, crowned it with jewels and a garland of flowers, carried it to the attic, and placed it as if to look out of the attic window. When everything was ready for the wedding, she dipped herself in a barrel of honey, then she cut open the featherbed and rolled in it until no one could recognize her, for she looked like a very strange bird. Then she left the house and on her way she met some of the wedding guests, who asked from where she came. "I come from the sorcerer's house," she replied.

"And how fares the young bride?" the guests asked. Through her feathered disguise, she answered, "From the bottom to the top, she is sweeping the house. See there, she is watching you from the attic window."

A little further on, she met her bridegroom, who was slowly returning home. He asked the same questions as his friends before him, and received the same answers. He looked up to the window, saw the decorated skull, and believed it to be his true bride. He kissed his hand lovingly to her and entered the house.

But just as he had gone in to greet his gathered guests, the brothers and other relatives of the bride arrived to rescue her. They locked up all the doors to the house so that no one could escape, and then set it afire, and the sorcerer and all his friends were burnt to ashes.

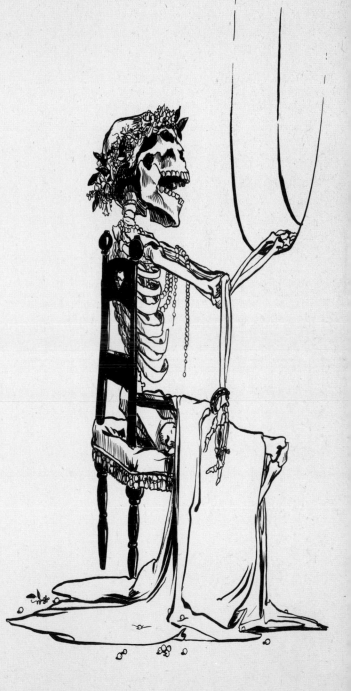

89

The Girl Without Hands

A CERTAIN MILLER had little by little fallen into poverty, and he had nothing left but his mill and a large apple tree that stood behind it. Once when he had gone into the forest to fetch wood, an old man stepped up to him whom he had never seen before, and said: "Why do you plague yourself with cutting wood? I will make you rich if you will promise me what is standing behind your mill."

"What can that be but my apple tree?" thought the miller, and said, "Yes," and he gave a written promise to the stranger. He, however, laughed mockingly and said, "When three years have passed, I will come and carry away what belongs to me," and then he went.

When the miller got home, his wife came to meet him and said: "Tell me, Miller, from whence comes this sudden wealth into our house? All at once every box and chest is filled; no one brought it in, and I know not how it happened."

He answered: "It comes from a stranger who met me in the forest and promised me great treasure. I, in return, have promised him what stands behind the mill; we can very well give him the big apple tree for it."

"Ah, husband," said the terrified wife, "that must have been the Devil! He did not mean the apple tree, but our daughter, who was standing behind the mill sweeping the yard."

The miller's daughter was a beautiful, pious girl, and she lived through the three years in the fear of God and without sin. When therefore the time was over, and the day came when the Devil was to fetch her, she washed herself clean and made a circle round herself with chalk. The Devil appeared very early, but he could not come near to her. Angrily, he said to the miller: "Take all water away from her, that she may no longer be able to wash herself, for otherwise I have no power over her." The miller was afraid, and did so.

The next morning the Devil came again, but she had wept on her hands, and they were absolutely clean. Again he could not get near her, and he furiously said to the miller: "Chop her hands off, or else I have no power over her."

The miller was terrified and answered: "How could I chop off my own child's hands?" Then the Devil threatened him and said: "If you do not do it, you are mine, and I will take you yourself."

The father became alarmed and promised to obey him. So he went to the girl and said: "My child, if I do not chop off both your hands, the Devil will carry me away, and in my terror I have promised to do it. Help me in my need, and forgive me the harm I do you."

She replied: "Dear Father, do with me what you will, I am your child." Thereupon she laid down both her hands and let them be cut off. The Devil came for the third time, but she had wept so long and so much on the stumps, that after all they were absolutely clean. Then he had to give in, and lost all right over her.

The miller said to her: "I have by means of you received such great wealth that I will keep you most handsomely as long as you live." But she replied: "Here I cannot stay, I will go forth; compassionate people will give me as much as I need." Thereupon she caused her maimed arms to be bound to her back, and by sunrise she set out on her way, and she walked the whole day until night fell.

Then she came to a royal garden, and by the shimmering of the moon she saw that trees covered with beautiful fruits grew in it, but she could not enter, for it was surrounded by water. And as she had walked the whole day and not eaten one mouthful, and hunger tormented her, she thought: "Ah, if I were but inside, that I might eat of the fruit, else must I die of hunger!" Then she knelt down and prayed to God. And suddenly an angel came toward her, who made a dam in the water, so that the moat became dry and she could walk through it.

And now she went into the garden and the angel went with her. She saw a tree covered with beautiful pears, but they were all counted. To still her hunger, she ate one with her mouth from the tree, but no more. The gardener was watching, but as the angel was standing by, he was afraid, and thought the maiden was a spirit, and was silent; neither did he dare to cry out or to speak to the spirit.

When she had eaten the pear, she was satisfied, and went and concealed herself among the bushes. The King to whom the garden belonged came down to it next morning, counted, and saw that one of the pears was missing. He asked the gardener what had become of it, as it was not lying beneath the tree, but was gone. Then answered the gardener: "Last night, a spirit came in, who had no hands, and ate off one of the pears with its mouth."

The King said: "How did the spirit get over the water, and where did it go after it had eaten the pear?" The gardener answered: "Someone came in a snow-white garment from heaven who made a dam, and kept back the water, that the spirit might walk through the moat. And as it must have been an angel, I was afraid, and asked no questions, and did not cry out. When the spirit had eaten the pear, it went back again." The King said: "If it be as you say, I will watch with you tonight."

When it grew dark, the King came into the garden and brought a priest with him, who was to speak to the spirit. All three seated themselves beneath the tree and watched. At midnight the maiden came creeping out of the thicket, went to the tree, and again ate one pear off it with her mouth, and beside her stood the angel in white garments. Then the priest went out to them and said: "Do you come from heaven or from earth? Are you a spirit, or a human being?" She replied: "I am no spirit, but a poor mortal deserted by all but God." The King said: "If you are forsaken by all the world, yet will I not forsake you." He took her with him into his royal palace, and as she was so beautiful and pious, he loved her with all his heart, had silver hands made for her, and took her to wife.

After a year the King had to go on a journey, so he commended his young Queen to the care of his mother, and said: "If she is brought to child-bed, take care of her, nurse her well, and tell me of it at once in a letter."

She gave birth to a fine boy, so the old mother made haste to write and announce the joyful news to the King. But the messenger rested by a brook on the way, and as he was fatigued by the great distance, he fell asleep. Then came the Devil, who was always seeking to harm the pious Queen, and exchanged the letter for another, in which was written that the Queen had brought a deformed child into the world.

When the King read the letter he was shocked and much troubled, but he wrote in answer that they were to take great care of the Queen and nurse her well until his arrival. The messenger went back with the letter, but rested at the same place and again fell asleep. Then came the Devil once more, and put a different letter in his pocket, in which it was written that they were to kill the Queen and her child. The old mother was terribly shocked when she received the letter and could not believe it. She wrote back again to the King, but received no other answer, because each time the Devil substituted a false letter, and in the last letter it was also written that she was to preserve the Queen's tongue and eyes as a token.

But the old mother wept to think such innocent blood was to be shed, and had a deer brought by night and cut out her tongue and eyes, and kept them. Then said she to the Queen: "I cannot have you killed as the King commands, but here you may stay no longer. Go forth into the wide world with your child, and never come here again."

The old Queen tied the child on her back and went away with eyes full of tears. She came into a great wild forest, and then she fell on her knees and prayed. An angel again appeared to her and led her to a little house on which was a sign with the words: "Here all dwell free." A snow-white maiden came out of the little house and said, "Welcome, Lady Queen," and conducted her inside. Then she unbound the little boy from her back, held him to her breast that he might feed, and laid him in a beautifully made little bed.

The Queen stayed seven years in the little house, and was well cared for, and because of her piety, her hands that had been cut off grew once more.

At last the King came home from his journey, and his first wish was to see his wife and the child. Then his aged mother began to weep and said, "You wicked man, why did you write to me that I was to take those two innocent lives?" She showed him the two letters which the Devil had forged, and then continued, "I did as you bade me," and she showed the tokens, the tongue and eyes.

Then the King began to weep for his poor wife and his little son so much more bitterly

than she was doing that the aged mother had compassion on him and said: "Be at peace, she still lives; I secretly caused a deer to be killed and took these tokens from it. But I bound the child to your wife's back and bade her go forth into the wide world, and made her promise never to come back here again because you were so angry with her."

Spoke the King: "I will go as far as the sky is blue, and will neither eat nor drink until I have found again my dear wife and my child, if in the meantime they have not been killed or died of hunger."

Thereupon the King traveled about for seven long years, and sought her in every cleft of the rocks and in every cave, but he found her not, and thought she had died of want. During the whole of this time he neither ate nor drank, but God supported him.

At length he came into a great forest and found therein the little house whose sign was, "Here all dwell free." Then forth came the white maiden, took him by the hand, led him in, and said: "Welcome, Lord King." The angel offered him meat and drink, but he did not take anything, and only wished to rest a little. Then he lay down to sleep.

Thereupon the angel went into the chamber where the Queen sat with her son, and said to her: "Go out with your child, your husband has come." Seeing them, the King rose and asked who they were. Then said she: "I am your wife, and that is your son, Sorrowful."

But he saw her living hands, and said: "My wife had silver hands." She answered him: "The good God has caused my natural hands to grow again." Whereupon the angel brought forth the silver hands and showed them to him. The King then knew for a certainty that it was his dear wife and his dear child, and he kissed them and was glad, and said: "A heavy stone has fallen from off my heart."

They went home to the King's aged mother, and there were great rejoicings everywhere. The King and Queen were married again, and lived contentedly to their happy end.

Allerleirauh

ANY YEARS HAVE PASSED since there lived a King who was married to the most beautiful woman in the world. She had hair of pure gold and together they had a daughter who was just as beautiful as her mother, and with hair just as golden. It came to pass that the Queen became quite ill and when she was about to die she called her husband to her side and made him promise that after she was dead he would not remarry unless he could find a woman who was as beautiful as she and had the same golden hair. When the King promised her this, she closed her eyes and died.

The King was so saddened by her death that for a long time he did not think of taking a second wife, but finally his royal advisors insisted that the kingdom needed a Queen. So the King sent for princesses from far and wide, but none was as beautiful as the queen who had died, and of course, there was not one with hair of gold.

One day the King took notice of his daughter and saw that she had grown to look exactly like her mother and had the same golden hair. The King thought to himself, "I will never find anyone in all the world more beautiful than my daughter. I will marry her and she will become my queen." The King felt so great a love for his daughter that he at once proclaimed his wishes to his advisors and to the Princess herself. The advisors were shocked, but their efforts to dissuade him were in vain.

The Princess was horrified at her father's wicked plan, but she was a clever girl and hoped to delay the marriage until he came to his senses. She told the King that she would marry him, but he must first give her three dresses: one as golden as the sun, one as silvery as the moon, and one that glittered like the stars. She must also have a coat made of a thousand different kinds of fur, and every animal in the kingdom would have to give up a piece of its hide for it.

The King's desire for his daughter was so fierce that he put his whole kingdom to work. The most talented seamstresses had to weave and sew the three gowns, and the huntsmen had to trap every kind of animal and skin it. It wasn't long before the King brought the Princess what she had wished for, and demanded that she marry him the next day.

The Princess now saw no hope of turning her father's heart, so she resolved to run away. That night she gathered up three presents from her betrothed—a gold ring, a tiny golden spinning wheel, and a little golden hook—and put the dresses of the sun, the moon, and the stars into a walnut shell; then she blackened her face and hands with soot, put on her coat of a thousand furs, and ran away. All night she walked until she came to a great forest where she would be safe, and because she was tired, she climbed into the hollow of a tree and fell asleep.

The sun rose the next morning and still the Princess slept. It happened that the King to whom she was betrothed was hunting nearby and his dogs came and ran around the tree and sniffed at it. The King sent his huntsmen to see what kind of animal might be hiding in the tree and they came back and said it was the most peculiar animal they had ever seen in all their lives. Its skin was made of a thousand different furs and it was lying there fast asleep. The King gave orders for the animal to be caught and tied on the back of the wagon, but as the huntsmen grabbed onto the creature, they saw that it was really a young girl and they tied her onto the back of the wagon and took her home with them, calling her Allerleirauh because of her patchwork pelt.

"Allerleirauh," they said, "you'll work in the kitchen. You can carry wood and water and sweep up the ashes." And they gave her a little stall under the stair, where no daylight ever came. "Here's where you can live and sleep," they told her. The poor Princess had to work in the kitchen and help the cook: she plucked the chickens, raked the fire, cleaned the vegetables, and did all the dirty work. She worked so neatly that the cook was pleased with her and some evenings he called Allerleirauh and gave her leftovers to eat. But before the King went to bed she had to go upstairs to take off his boots and it always

happened that when she had one boot taken off, the King would throw it at her head. Allerleirauh lived in this wretched way for a long time.

Then it happened that there was a festival held in the palace. Allerleirauh went to the cook and asked if he wouldn't let her go upstairs for a while and stand at the door to look in on all the dancing. "Go, then," he said, "but be back in a half-hour to sweep the hearth." Allerleirauh took her oil lamp and

went to her little stall, and washed the soot off her face and hands; then she took off her coat of fur, opened the walnut shell, and took out the dress that shone like the sun. And when she was all dressed she went to the festival and everybody made way for her, assuming her to be a king's daughter.

The King took her hand at once and as they were danc-ing he thought, "How this beautiful, strange princess resembles my dear bride." The longer he looked at her, the more the resemblance grew. He was going to ask who she was when the dance was over, but Allerleirauh curtsied quickly, and when the King looked round again, she had vanished and no one saw where she went. He sent to question the watchmen, but none had seen the Princess leave the palace.

Meanwhile, Allerleirauh had run to her lit-tle stall, quickly taken off her dress, black-ened her face and hands, and put her coat of fur back on. She went into the kitchen and began sweeping the ashes, but the cook said, "Leave the sweeping until tomorrow and come make some soup for the King. I, too, want to go and see the dancing, but don't let a hair fall into the pot or I'll never give you anything to eat again." So Allerleirauh cooked the King a bread soup and when it was done she placed the golden ring that he had given her in the bowl.

When the dancing was over, the King asked for his bread soup and after he had eaten it he thought that he had never tasted better. When he found the golden ring lying at the bottom of the bowl, he looked at it closely and saw that it was his wedding ring. Astonished and not understanding how it had got there, he called for the cook. When the cook heard the order, he turned angrily to Allerleirauh and said, "If you have let a hair fall in the soup, I'm going to beat you." But when the cook came upstairs, the King asked who had cooked the soup because it was better than usual. When the cook confessed that Allerleirauh had made it, she was sent for as well.

When Allerleirauh came before the King, he asked, "Who are you?" "I am a poor girl who no longer has any father or mother," she replied. "Of what use are you in my palace?" asked the King. "I am good for nothing but to have boots thrown at my head," she said. And when the King asked her: "Where did you get the ring that was in my soup?" Aller-leirauh answered, "I know nothing about the ring," and ran away.

After that there was another festival and again Allerleirauh asked the cook to let her go upstairs. The cook let her go but only for a half-hour and then she was to come back and cook the King his bread soup. Allerleirauh ran to her little stall, washed herself clean, and took out the dress that was as silvery as the moon, and when she came upstairs the dance was just beginning. The King gave her his hand and danced with her and no longer doubted that this was his bride because no one else in all the world had such golden hair. But when the dance was over, she again disappeared so quickly that no one saw where she went. Meanwhile, Allerleirauh had donned her coat of a thousand furs, blackened her face and hands, and stood in the kitchen cooking the King's bread soup, while the cook had gone upstairs to watch the dancing. And when the soup was finished she put in the little golden spinning wheel. The King ate the soup and it seemed to him it tasted even better than before, and when he found the golden spinning wheel at the bottom he was even more astonished because it was the one he had given to his betrothed. The cook was sent for, and then Allerleirauh,

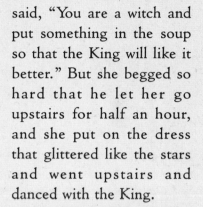

but again she answered that she was good for nothing else but to have boots thrown at her head, and that she knew nothing at all about the little golden spinning wheel.

For the third time the King held a festival and everything happened just as it had before. The cook scolded Allerleirauh and said, "You are a witch and put something in the soup so that the King will like it better." But she begged so hard that he let her go upstairs for half an hour, and she put on the dress that glittered like the stars and went upstairs and danced with the King.

It seemed to him that he had never seen her as beautiful as this. The King had ordered that the music should play for a very long time, and while they were dancing, he secretly slipped the golden ring onto her finger. When the dance had finally ended, he wanted to hold her fast, but she tore herself away from him, and ran so quickly through the crowd that she vanished from his sight.

She ran to her little stall, but had stayed too long and so had no time to take off her most beautiful dress and could only throw her coat of a thousand furs over it. In her hurry to blacken her face and hands, she left one

finger white, and when she came to the kitchen the cook was already gone. Allerleirauh quickly cooked the bread soup and added the golden hook. The King found it, as he had the ring and the spinning wheel. Now he was sure that his bride was near—she alone could have had these presents. Allerleirauh was summoned and the King saw her white finger, the one upon which he had placed the golden ring. He grasped her by the hand and held her fast, and when she tried to pull free and run away, her fur covering opened and the dress of stars shone through.

The King clutched at the fur mantle and tore it off. Then her golden hair shone even more brightly than her gown, and Allerleirauh stood there in full splendor, and could no longer hide herself. The King said to her, "You are my dear bride, and we will nevermore part from each other." After which their marriage was solemnized and they lived happily together until their death.

The Mother-in-Law

NCE UPON A TIME there lived a King and a Queen, and that Queen had a wickedly evil mother-in-law. When the King went off to war, the old Queen had her daughter-in-law locked up in a musty room in the cellar, and her two little boys were locked up with her. One day the old Queen found herself with a craving for human flesh and she thought, "I would love to eat one of those two little boys." Upon that thought, she summoned the cook and ordered him to fetch one of her grandsons from the cellar and have him slaughtered and prepared for cooking. "What kind of sauce should I prepare?" asked the cook. "A brown one," replied the old Queen.

The cook went down to the cellar and said: "Oh my Queen, the old Queen wants me to slaughter and cook your son tonight." The young Queen was deeply distressed and said: "Why can't we take a baby pig instead? You can cook it just as she wanted and tell her that it's my child."

The cook did just that and presented the roasted suckling in a brown sauce: "Here is the child." And the old Queen ate it with a hearty appetite.

Soon after, the old woman thought to herself, "The flesh of that child was so delicate and tasty, I'll just have to eat the other one, too." So she again summoned the cook, sent him to the cellar, and commanded him to slaughter the second child. "In what kind of sauce should I cook him?" "A white one," replied the old Queen.

The cook went down to the cellar and said: "Now the old Queen has ordered me to slaughter and cook your second little son." The young Queen again begged of the cook: "Take a suckling pig and cook it the way she likes it." So the cook did just that and presented the suckling pig to the old woman in a white sauce as she had requested, and she ate it with an even heartier appetite.

At last, the old woman thought to herself, "Now the children are in my body, and I can eat the young Queen herself." She summoned the cook and ordered that the young Queen be made for her dinner. When asked how she should be prepared, the old Queen replied, "Well spiced."

Once more the cook went to the cellar and spoke to his Queen. A suckling pig would not fool the old woman this time, but she told him to prepare a young deer just brought in from the hunt instead. Again, the cook did as she said and brought to the table a well-spiced venison, which the old Queen ate with the heartiest appetite of all.

Oh! Just imagine the plight of the poor young Queen, locked away in the cellar with her two young Princes. As time went on and her husband did not return, it was more and more difficult to keep the little boys from their fussing and crying.

It then came to pass that the old Queen, her appetite piqued, would roam the halls of the castle in the dead of night, hoping to pick up the scent of a tender young servant child who should be hers for the eating. As the old woman crept quietly through the cellar one night, she heard a baby's sudden wail and knew at once that the young Queen and the Princes still lived.

Enraged at the cook's deception, the old woman ordered a large cauldron to be brought forth and filled to the top with vipers, toads, and serpents. Then were the cook, the young Queen, and her two sons brought before her and she prepared to throw them all into the pot to meet their death.

It happened that just as the old woman's victims were about to be tossed into the slithering stew, there came a clattering of horses in the castle courtyard. Then the old Queen knew that the King had returned from battle and he would surely see her punished for her wicked appetites.

So afraid was the old woman of what his revenge would hold in store that she threw herself into the deadly cauldron and was quickly eaten up by the writhing, snapping reptiles. When the King heard of the old woman's death, he allowed himself a brief moment of mourning, for she was—after all—his very own mother. Then he gathered his Queen and his two sons to his breast and was joyous and thankful for their lives.

The Dog and the Sparrow

⬧⬧⬧

OME TIME AGO THERE WAS a sheep dog whose master behaved ill to him and did not give him enough to eat, and when for hunger he could bear it no longer, he left his service very sadly. In the street he was met by a sparrow, who said, "Dog, my brother, why are you so sad?" And the dog answered, "I am hungry and have nothing to eat." Said the sparrow, "Dear brother, come with me into the town; I will give you plenty."

Then they went together into the town, and soon they came to a butcher's stall, and the sparrow said to the dog, "Stay here while I peck you down a piece of meat," and he perched on the stall, looked round to see that no one noticed him, and pecked, pulled, and dragged so long at a piece that lay near the edge of the board that at last it slid to the ground. The dog picked it up, ran with it into a corner, and ate it up. Then said the sparrow, "Now come with me to another stall, and I will get you another piece, so that your hunger may be satisfied."

When the dog had devoured a second piece, the sparrow asked, "Dog, my brother, are you satisfied now?" "Yes, as to meat I am," answered he, "but I have had no bread." Then said the sparrow, "That also shall you have; come with me."

And he led him to a baker's stall and pecked at a few rolls until they rolled to the ground, and as the dog still wanted more, they went to another stall farther on and got more bread. When that was eaten up the sparrow said, "Dog, my brother, are you satisfied yet?" "Yes," answered he, "and now we will walk a little outside the town."

And they went together along the high road. It was warm weather, and when they had gone a little way the dog said, "I am tired, and would like to go to sleep." "Well, do so," said the sparrow. "In the meanwhile I will sit on a bough."

The dog laid himself in the road and fell fast asleep, and as he lay there a wagoner came up with a wagon and three horses, laden with two casks of wine; the sparrow, seeing that the wagoner was not going to turn aside, but kept in the beaten track just where the dog lay, cried out, "Wagoner, take care, or I shall make you poor!"

But the wagoner, muttering, "You won't make me poor!" cracked his whip and pushed his wagon over the dog, and he was crushed to death by the wheels. Then the sparrow cried, "Thou hast killed the dog, my brother, and it shall cost thee horse and cart!"

"Why! Horse and cart!" said the wagoner. "What harm can you do me?" and drove on. The sparrow crept under the wagon cover and pecked at the bung hole of one of the casks until the cork came out, and all the wine ran out without the wagoner noticing. After a while, looking round, he saw that something dripped from the wagon, and on examining the casks he found that one of them was empty, and he cried out, "Ah, poor man that I am!"

"Not poor enough yet!" said the sparrow, and flying to one of the horses he perched on

his head and pecked at his eyes. When the wagoner saw that, he took out his ax to hit the sparrow, who at that moment flew aloft, and the wagoner missing him struck the horse on the head, so that he fell down dead. "Ah, poor man that I am!" cried he.

"Not poor enough yet!" said the sparrow, and as the wagoner drove on with the two horses that were left, the sparrow crept again under the wagon cover and pecked the cork out of the second cask, so that all the wine

leaked out. When the wagoner became aware of it, he cried out again, "Ah, poor man that I am!" But the sparrow answered, "Not poor enough yet!" and perched on the second horse's head and began pecking at his eyes. Back ran the wagoner and raised his ax to strike, but the sparrow flew aloft and the stroke fell on the horse, so that he was killed.

"Ah, poor man that I am!" cried the wagoner. "Not poor enough yet!" said the sparrow, and perching on the third horse began pecking at his eyes. The wagoner struck out in his anger at the sparrow without taking aim, and missing him, he laid his third horse dead.

"Ah, poor man that I am!" he cried. "Not poor enough yet!" said the sparrow, flying off: "Now I will make you poor at home."

So the wagoner had to leave his wagon standing, and went home full of rage. "Oh!" said he to his wife, "what ill luck I have had! The wine is spilled, and the horses are all three dead."

"Oh husband!" answered she, "such a wicked bird has come to this house; he has brought with him all the birds of the world, and there they fell upon our wheat and devoured it." And he looked and there were thousands upon thousands of birds sitting on the ground, having eaten up all the wheat, and the sparrow in the midst, and the wagoner cried, "Ah, poor man that I am!" "Not poor enough yet!" answered the sparrow. "Wagoner, it shall cost thee thy life!" and he flew away.

Now the wagoner had lost everything he possessed, and he went indoors and sat down angry and miserable behind the stove. The sparrow was perched outside on the windowsill, and cried, "Wagoner, it shall cost thee thy life!" Then the wagoner seized his ax and threw it at the sparrow, but it broke the window sash in two and did not touch the sparrow. He now hopped inside, perched on the stove, and cried, "Wagoner, it shall cost thee thy life!" and he, mad and blind with rage, beat the stove in two, and as the sparrow flew from one spot to another, he hacked everything in pieces—furniture, looking glasses, benches, table, and the very walls of his house—and yet did not touch the sparrow.

At last he caught and held him in his hand. "Now," said his wife, "shall I not kill him?"

"No!" cried he, "that were too easy a death; he shall be murdered more cruelly. I will swallow him." And he swallowed the sparrow whole. And as the bird fluttered in the man's body, it stretched out its head and said, "Wagoner, it shall cost thee thy life!"

Then the wagoner reached the ax to his wife, saying, "Wife, strike me this bird dead." The wife struck, but missed her aim, and the blow fell on the wagoner's head, and he dropped down dead. But the sparrow flew over the hills and away.

Rapunzel

MAN AND A WOMAN had long in vain wished for a child. At length the woman hoped that God was about to grant her desire. These people had a little window at the back of their house from which a splendid garden could be seen, which was full of the most beautiful flowers and herbs. It was, however, surrounded by a high wall, and no one dared to go into it because it belonged to an enchantress, who had great power and was dreaded by all the world.

One day the woman was standing by this window and looking down into the garden, when she saw a bed that was planted with the most beautiful rampion, and the leaves looked so fresh and green that she longed for it and had the greatest desire to eat some. This desire increased every day, and as she knew that she could not get any of it, she quite pined away and began to look pale and miserable.

Then her husband was alarmed, and asked: "What ails you, dear wife?" "Ah," she replied, "if I can't eat some of the rampion that is in the garden behind our house, I shall die." The man, who loved her very much, thought, "Sooner than let your wife die, bring her some of the rampion yourself; let it cost what it will."

At twilight, he climbed over the wall into the garden of the enchantress, hastily clutched a handful of rampion, and took it to his wife. She at once made herself a salad of it, and ate it greedily. It tasted so good to her—so very good that the next day she longed for it three times as much as before. If she was to have any rest, her husband must once more descend into the garden. In the gloom of evening, therefore, he let himself down again; but when he had clambered down the wall he was terrified, for he saw the enchantress standing before him.

"How can you dare," said she, "descend into my garden and steal my rampion like a thief? You shall suffer for it!" "Ah," answered he, "I only made up my mind to do it out of necessity. My wife saw your rampion from the window, and felt such a

longing for it that she would have died if she had not got some to eat."

Then the enchantress allowed her anger to be softened, and said to him: "If the case be as you say, I will allow you to take away with you as much rampion as you will, only I make one condition: you must give me the child which your wife will bring into the world; it shall be well treated, and I will care for it like a mother." The man in his terror consented to everything, and when the woman was brought to bed, the enchantress appeared at once, gave the child the name of Rapunzel, and took it away with her.

Rapunzel grew into the most beautiful child under the sun. When she was twelve years old, the enchantress shut her into a tower, which lay in a forest and had neither stairs nor door, but quite at the top was a little window. When the enchantress wanted to go in, she placed herself beneath it and cried—

"Rapunzel, Rapunzel,
Let down your hair to me."

Rapunzel had long, magnificent hair, fine as spun gold, and when she heard the voice of the enchantress, she unfastened her braided tresses, wound them round one of the hooks of the window above, and then the hair fell twenty ells down, and the enchantress climbed up by it.

After a few years, it came to pass that the King's son rode through the forest and passed by the tower. Then he heard a song, which was so charming that he stood still and listened. This was Rapunzel, who in her solitude passed her time in letting her sweet voice resound. The King's son looked in vain for the door of the tower. But the singing had so deeply touched his heart that every day he went out into the forest and listened to it. Once when he was thus standing behind a tree, he saw that the enchantress came there, and he heard how she cried—

"Rapunzel, Rapunzel,
Let down your hair to me."

Then Rapunzel let down the braids of her hair, and the enchantress climbed up to her. "If that is the ladder by which one mounts, I, too, will try my fortune," said he, and the next day when it began to grow dark, he went to the tower and cried—

"Rapunzel, Rapunzel,
Let down your hair to me."

Soon the hair fell down, and the King's son climbed up.

At first Rapunzel was terribly frightened when a man, such as her eyes had never yet beheld, came to her, but the King's son began to talk to her quite like a friend, and he told her that his heart had been so stirred that it had let him have no rest, and he had been forced to see her. Rapunzel lost her fear, and soon she came to like the King's son so much that she agreed to let him visit every day and to pull him up. The two lived joyfully for a time, and when he asked if Rapunzel would take him for her husband, she said yes, and laid her hand in his. "I will willingly go away with you," she said, "but I do not know how to get down. Bring with you a skein of silk every time that you come, and I will weave a ladder with it, and when that is ready I will descend, and you will take me on your horse."

They agreed that until that time he should come to her every evening, for the old woman came by day. The enchantress noticed nothing at all of this, until once Rapunzel said to her: "Tell me, Godmother, why my clothes are so tight and why they don't fit me any longer?" "Ah! you wicked child," cried the enchantress. "What do I see before me! I thought I had separated you from all the world, and yet you have deceived me!"

In her anger she clutched Rapunzel's beautiful tresses, wrapped them a few times round her left hand, seized a pair of scissors with the right, and—snip-snap!—they were cut off, and the lovely braids lay on the ground. And she was so merciless that she took poor Rapunzel in a waste and desert where she lived in great woe and misery.

On the same day that she cast out Rapunzel, however, the enchantress fastened the braids of hair, which she had cut off, to the hook of the window, and when the King's son came and cried—

"Rapunzel, Rapunzel,
Let down your hair to me—"

she let the hair down. The King's son ascended, but instead of finding his dearest Rapunzel, he found the enchantress, who gazed at him with wicked and venomous eyes. "Aha!" she cried mockingly, "Rapunzel is lost to you; you will never see her again."

The King's son was beside himself with pain, and in his despair he leapt down from the tower. He escaped with his life, but the thorns into which he fell pierced his eyes. Then he wandered blind about the forest, ate nothing but roots and berries, and did naught but lament and weep over the loss of his dearest wife. Thus he roamed about in misery for some years, and at length came to the desert where Rapunzel, with the twins that she had borne, a boy and a girl, lived in wretchedness.

He heard a voice, and it seemed so familiar to him that he went toward it, and when he approached, Rapunzel knew him and fell on his neck and wept. Two of her tears wet his eyes, and they grew clear again, and he could see with them as before. He led her to his kingdom, where he was joyfully received, and they lived for a long time afterward, happy and contented.

Little Brother and Little Sister

HE BROTHER TOOK his sister's hand and said to her, "Since our mother died we have had no good days. Our stepmother beats us every day, and if we come to her, she kicks us away with her feet. We have nothing to eat but hard crusts of bread left over; the dog under the table fares better; he gets a good piece every now and then. If our mother only knew, how she would pity us! Come, let us go together out into the wide world!"

So they went and journeyed the whole day through fields and meadows and stony places, and if it rained, the sister said, "The skies and we are weeping together." In the evening they came to a great wood, and they were so weary with hunger and their long journey that they sat down in a hollow tree and fell asleep.

The next morning, when they awoke, the sun was high in heaven and shone brightly into the tree. Then said the brother, "Sister, I am thirsty; if I only knew where to find a well, that I might go and drink! I think that I hear one rushing." So the brother got up and took his sister by the hand, and they went to seek the well. But their wicked stepmother was a witch and had known quite well that the two children had gone away, and she had sneaked after them, secretly as only witches can do, and had laid a spell on all the wells in the forest. So when they found a little well, the brother was going to drink of it, but the sister heard how it said in its rushing—

"He a tiger will be who drinks of me, / who drinks of me a tiger will be!"

Then the sister cried, "Pray, dear brother, do not drink, or you will become a wild beast, and will tear me to pieces." So the brother refrained from drinking, though his thirst was great, and he said he would wait till he came to the next well. When they

came to a second well the sister heard it say in its rushing—

"He a wolf will be who drinks of me,
Who drinks of me a wolf will be!"

Then the sister cried, "Pray, dear brother, do not drink, or you will be turned into a wolf, and will eat me up!" So the brother refrained from drinking, and said, "I will wait until the next well, and then I must drink, whatever you say; my thirst is so great." And when they came to the third well the sister heard how in its rushing it said—

"Who drinks of me a
fawn will be,
He a fawn will be who
drinks of me!"

Then the sister said, "Oh my brother, I pray drink not, or you will be turned into a fawn, and run away far from me." But he had already knelt by the side of the well and stooped and drunk of the water, and as the first drops passed his lips he became a fawn.

And the sister wept over her poor cursed brother, and the fawn wept also and stayed sadly beside her. At last the maiden said, "Be comforted, dear fawn, indeed I will never leave you." Then she untied her golden girdle and bound it round the fawn's neck, and went and gathered rushes to make a soft cord, which she fastened to him; and then she led him on, and they went deeper into the forest. And when they had gone a long, long way, they came at last to a little house, and the maiden looked inside, and as it was empty, she thought, "We might as well stay and live here."

And she fetched leaves and moss to make a soft bed for the fawn, and every morning she went out and gathered roots and berries and nuts for herself, and fresh grass for the fawn, who ate out of her hand with joy, frolicking round her. At night, when the sister was tired and had said her prayers, she laid her head on the fawn's back, which served her for a pillow, and softly fell asleep. And if only the brother could have got back his own shape again, it would have been a charming life. So they lived a long while in the wilderness alone.

Now it happened that the King of that country held a great hunt in the forest. The blowing of the horns, the barking of the dogs, and the lusty shouts of the huntsmen sounded throughout the wood, and the fawn heard them and was eager to be among them.

"Oh," said he to his sister, "do let me go to the hunt; I cannot stay behind any longer," and he begged so long that at last she consented.

"But mind," said she to him, "come back to me at night. I must lock my door against the wild hunters, so in order that I may know you, you must knock and say, 'Little sister, let me in,' and unless I hear that I shall not unlock the door."

Then the fawn sprang out and felt glad and merry in the open air. The King and his huntsmen saw the beautiful animal and began at once to pursue him, but they could not come within reach of him, for when they thought they were certain of him, he sprang away over the bushes and disappeared. As soon as it was dark he went back to the little house, knocked at the door, and said, "Little sister, let me in."

Then the door was opened to him, and he went in, and rested the whole night long on his soft bed. The next morning the hunt began anew, and when the fawn heard the hunting horns and the tally-ho of the huntsmen, he could rest no longer, and said, "Little sister, let me out. I must go." The sister opened the door and said, "Now, mind you must come back at night and say the same words."

When the King and his hunters saw the fawn with the golden collar again, they chased him closely, but he was too nimble and swift for them. This lasted the whole day, and at last the hunters surrounded him, and one of them wounded his foot a little, so that he was obliged to limp and to go slowly. Then a hunter slipped after him to the little house and heard how he called out, "Little sister, let me in," and saw the door

open and shut again after him directly. The hunter noticed all this carefully, went to the King, and told him all he had seen and heard. Then said the King, "Tomorrow we will hunt again."

But the sister was very terrified when she saw that her fawn come in wounded. She washed the blood, laid herbs round it, and said, "Lie down on your bed, dear fawn, and rest, that you may soon be well." The wound was very slight, so that the fawn felt nothing of it the next morning. And when he heard the noise of the hunting outside, he said, "I cannot stay in, I must be with them; I shall not be taken easily again!" The sister began to weep, and said, "I know you will be killed, and I left alone here in the forest and forsaken of everybody. I cannot let you go!"

"Then I shall die here with longing if you don't let me go," answered the fawn, "when I hear the sound of the horn I feel as if I should leap out of my skin." Then the sister saw there was no help for it, unlocked the door with a heavy heart, and the fawn bounded away into the forest, well and merry. When the King saw him, he said to his hunters, "Now, follow him up all day long till the night comes, and see that you do him no hurt." So as soon as the sun had gone down, the King said to the huntsman: "Now, come and show me the little house in the wood."

And when he got to the door he knocked at it and cried, "Little sister, let me in!"

Then the door opened, and the King went in, and there stood a maiden more beautiful than any he had seen before. The maiden shrieked out when she saw, instead of the fawn, a man standing there with a gold crown on his head. But the King looked kindly on her, gave her his hand, and said, "Will you go with me to my castle and be my dear wife?"

"Ah, yes," answered the maiden, "but the fawn must come, too. I do not leave him." And the King said, "He shall remain with you as long as you live, and shall lack nothing." Then the fawn came bounding in, and the sister tied the cord of rushes to him, and led him by her own hand out of the little house.

The King led the beautiful maiden to his castle, where the wedding was held with great pomp; so she became lady Queen, and they lived together happily for a long while. The fawn was well tended and cherished, and he gamboled about the castle garden.

Now the wicked stepmother, whose fault it was that the children were driven out into the world, never dreamed but that the sister had been eaten up by wild beasts in the forest, and that the brother, in the likeness of a fawn, had been slain by the hunters. But when she heard that they were so happy, and that things had gone so well with them, jealousy and envy arose in her heart and pinched it and nibbled at it, and her chief thought was how to bring misfortune on her stepchildren.

Her own daughter, who was ugly as the night and had only one eye, complained to her, and said, "It would be fit for me to have become a queen." "Never mind," said the old woman, to satisfy her. "When the time comes, I shall be at hand."

After a while the Queen brought a beautiful baby boy into the world, and that day the King was out hunting. The old witch took the shape of the bedchamber woman, and she went into the room where the Queen lay, and said to her, "Come, the bath is ready; it will give you refreshment and new strength. Quick, or it will be cold."

The old woman's daughter was at hand, so they carried the weak Queen into the bathroom and laid her down there and left quickly and locked the door. And in the bathroom they had made a great fire, so as to suffocate the beautiful young Queen.

When that was managed, the old woman took her daughter, put a cap on her, and laid her in the bed in the Queen's place, gave her also the Queen's form and countenance, only she could not restore the lost eye. So, in order that the King might not remark it, she had to lie on the side where there was no eye. In the evening, when the King came home and heard that a little son was born to him, he rejoiced with all his heart and went at once to his dear wife's bedside to see how she did. Then the old woman cried hastily, "For your life, do not draw back the curtains to let in the light upon her; she must be kept quiet." So the King went away and never knew that a false Queen was lying in the bed.

Now, when it was midnight, and everyone was asleep, the nurse, who was sitting by the cradle in the nursery and watching there alone, saw the door open and the true Queen come in. She took the child out of the cradle, laid it to her bosom, and fed it. Then she shook out his little pillow, put the child back again, and covered it with the coverlet. She did not forget the fawn either: she went to him where he lay in the corner and stroked his back tenderly. Then she went in perfect silence out the door, and the nurse next morning asked the watchmen if anyone had entered the castle during the night, but they said they had seen no one. And the

Queen came many nights and never said a word; the nurse saw her always, but she did not dare speak of it to anyone.

After some time had gone by in this manner, the Queen seemed to find voice, and said one night—

"My child, my fawn, twice more I see,
Twice more, and then the end must be."

The nurse said nothing, but as soon as the Queen had disappeared, she went to the King and told him all. The King said, "Ah, heaven! What do I hear! I will myself watch by the child this very night!"

So that evening, he went into the nursery, and at midnight the Queen appeared and said—

"My child, my fawn, once more I see,
Once more, and then the end must be."

And she tended the child, as she was accustomed to do, before she vanished. The King dared not speak, but he watched again the following night, and heard her say—

"My child, my fawn, this once I see,
This once, and then the end must be."

Then the King could contain himself no longer, but rushed toward her and said, "You are no other than my dear wife!" Then she answered, "Yes, I am your dear wife," and in that moment, by the grace of heaven, her life returned to her, and she was once more fresh, real, and healthy. Then she told the King of the snare that the wicked witch and her daughter had laid for her. The King had them both brought to justice, and sentence was passed upon them.

The daughter was sent away into the wood, where she was devoured by the wild beasts, and the witch was burned, and ended miserably. And as soon as the fire had eaten her body, the spell was removed from the fawn, and he took human shape again; and the sister and brother lived happily together until their end.

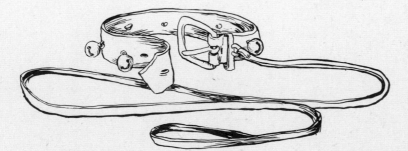

The Story of the Youth Who Went Forth to Learn How to Shudder

 CERTAIN FATHER had two sons, the elder of whom was smart and sensible and could do everything, but the younger was stupid and could neither learn nor understand anything, and when people saw him they said: "His father will have some trouble with him!" When anything had to be done, it was always the elder who was forced to do it. But if his father bade him fetch anything when it was late, or in the nighttime, and the way led through the churchyard or any other dismal place, he answered, "Oh, no, Father, I'll not go there, it makes me shudder!" for he was afraid. Or when stories were told by the fire at night that made the flesh creep, the listeners sometimes said: "Oh, it makes us shudder!" The younger sat in a corner and listened with the rest of them and could not grasp what they meant. "They are always saying: 'It makes me shudder, it makes me shudder!' It does not make me shudder," thought he. "That, too, must be an art of which I understand nothing!"

Now it came to pass that his father said to him one day: "Listen to me, you fellow in the corner there, you are growing tall and strong, and you, too, must learn something by which you can earn your bread. Look how your brother works, but you do not even earn your salt." "Well, Father," he replied, "I am quite willing to learn something—indeed, if it could but be managed, I should like to learn how to shudder. I don't understand that at all yet."

The elder brother laughed when he heard that, and thought to himself: "Good God, what a blockhead that brother of mine is! He will never be good for anything as long as I live! He who wants to be a sickle must bend himself."

The father sighed, and answered him: "You shall soon learn what it is to shudder, but you will not earn your bread by that."

Soon after this the sexton came to the house on a visit, and the father bewailed his trouble and told him how his younger son was so backward in every respect that he knew nothing and learned nothing. "Just think," said he, "when I asked him how he was going to earn his bread, he actually wanted to learn how to shudder." "If that be all," replied the sexton, "he can learn with me, and I will soon polish him." The father was glad to do it, for he thought: "It will train the boy a little."

The sexton therefore took him into his house, and he had to ring the church bell. After a few days, the sexton awoke him at midnight and bade him arise and go up into the church tower and ring the bell. "You shall soon learn what shuddering is," thought he, and in order to terrify him secretly went there before him and positioned himself where the boy should take him for a ghost; and when the boy was at the top of the tower, he saw a figure standing by the sounding hole. "Who is there?" cried he, but the figure did not move or stir. "Give an answer," cried the boy, "or take yourself off, or I'll push you down."

The sexton, however, remained standing motionless that the boy might think he was a ghost. The boy cried a second time: "What do you want here at night? Speak if you are an honest fellow, or I will throw you down the steps!" The sexton thought, "He can't mean to be as bad as his words," and he so he uttered no sound and stood as if he were made of stone. Then the boy called to the ghost for the third time, and as that was also to no purpose, he ran against it and pushed the ghost down so that it broke its neck. Thereupon he rang the bell, went home, and without saying a word went to bed and fell asleep.

The sexton's wife waited a long time for her husband, but he did not come back. At length she became uneasy, and wakened the boy, and asked: "Do you not know where my husband is? He climbed up the tower before you did." "No, I don't know," replied the boy, "but someone was standing by the sounding hole, and as he would neither give an answer nor go away, I took him for a scoundrel and threw him down. Just go there and you will see if it was he." The woman ran to the churchyard and found her husband dead on the ground.

Then with loud screams she hastened to the boy's father and woke him up. "Your good-for-nothing boy," cried she, "has been the cause of a great misfortune! He has

thrown my husband down the sounding hole so that he is dead in the churchyard." The father was terrified, and ran thither and scolded the boy. "What wicked tricks are these?" said he, "the Devil must have put them into your head." "Father," he replied, "I am quite innocent. He was standing there by night like one intent on doing evil. I did not know who it was, and I entreated him three times—why didn't he answer me?" "Ah," said the father, "I have nothing but unhappiness with you. Go out of my sight. I don't want to see you no more."

"Yes, Father, right willingly; wait only until it is day. Then will I go forth and learn how to shudder, and then I shall, at any rate, understand one art that will feed me." "Learn what you will," spoke the father, "it is all the same to me. Here are fifty talers for you. Take these and get out of my sight. Tell no one from whence you come, and who is your father, for I have reason to be ashamed of you." "Yes, Father, it shall be as you will. If you desire nothing more than that, I can easily keep it in mind."

When day dawned, therefore, the boy put his fifty talers into his pocket and went forth on the great highway, and he continually said to himself: "If I could but shudder! If I could but shudder!" Then a man approached who heard this conversation, and when they had walked a little farther to where they could see the gallows, the man said to him: "Look, there is the tree where seven men have mar-

ried the rope maker's daughter. Sit down beneath it and wait till night comes, and you will soon learn how to shudder."

"If that is all that is wanted," answered the youth, "it is easily done, but if I learn how to shudder as fast as that, you shall have my fifty talers. Just come back to me early in the morning." Then the youth went to the gallows, sat down beneath it, and waited till evening came. And as he was cold, he lighted himself a fire, but at midnight the wind blew so sharply that in spite of his fire, he could not get warm. And as the wind knocked the hanged men against one another, and they moved backward and forward, he thought to himself: "If you shiver below by the fire, how those up above must freeze and flounder!" And as he felt pity for them, he raised the ladder, climbed up, unbound one of them after the other, and brought down all seven. Then he stoked the fire, blew it, and set them all round it to warm themselves.

But they sat there and did not stir, and the fire caught their clothes. So he said: "Take care, or I will hang you up again." The dead men, however, did not hear, were quite silent, and let their rags go on burning. At this he grew angry, and said: "If you will not take care, I cannot help you. I will not be burnt with you." And he hung them up again each in his turn. Then he sat down by his fire and fell asleep, and the next morning the man came to him and wanted to have the talers, and said: "Well, do you know how to shudder?" "No," answered he, "how should I know? Those fellows up there did not open their mouths, and they were so stupid that they let the few old rags that they had on their bodies get burnt." Then the man saw that he would not get the fifty talers that day, and went away saying: "Such a youth has never come my way before."

The youth likewise went his way, and once more began to mutter to himself: "Ah, if I could but shudder! Ah, if I could but shudder!" A wagoner who was striding behind him heard this and asked: "Who are you?" "I don't know," answered the youth. Then the wagoner asked: "From whence do you come?" "I know not." "Who is your father?" "That I may not tell you." "What is it that you are always muttering between your teeth?" "Ah," replied the youth, "I do so wish I could shudder, but no one can teach me how." "Enough of your foolish chatter," said the wagoner. "Come, go with me, I will see about a place for you."

The youth went with the wagoner, and in the evening they arrived at an inn where they wished to pass the night. Then at the entrance of the parlor the youth again said quite loudly, "If I could but shudder! If I could but shudder!" The innkeeper who heard this laughed and said: "If that is your

desire, there ought to be a good opportunity for you here." "Ah, be silent," said the innkeeper's wife, "so many who were inquisitive have already lost their lives. It would be a pity and a shame if such beautiful eyes as these should never see the daylight again."

But the youth said: "However difficult it may be, I will learn it. For this purpose indeed have I journeyed forth." He let the innkeeper have no rest until the latter told him that not far from thence stood a haunted castle where anyone could very easily learn what shuddering was, if he would but watch in it for three nights. The King had promised that he who would venture this should have his daughter to wife, and she was the most beautiful maiden that the sun shone upon. Likewise, in the castle lay great treasures, which were guarded by spirits, and these treasures would then be freed and would make a poor man rich enough. Already many men had gone into the castle, but as yet none had come out again.

Then the youth went next morning to the King, and said: "If it be allowed, I will willingly watch three nights in the haunted castle." The King looked at him, and as the youth pleased him, he said: "You may ask for three things to take into the castle with you, but they must be things without life." The youth answered: "Then I ask for a fire, a turning lathe, and a cutting board with the knife."

The King had these things carried into the castle for him during the day. When night was drawing near, the youth went up and made himself a bright fire in one of the rooms, placed the cutting board and knife beside it, and seated himself by the turning lathe. "Ah, if I could but shudder!" said he, "but I shall not learn it here either."

Toward midnight he was about to poke his fire, and as he was blowing it, something cried suddenly from one corner: "Oh, mee-oww! How cold we are!"

"You fools!" cried he, "what are you crying about? If you are cold, come and take a seat by the fire and warm yourselves." And when he had said that, two great black cats came with one tremendous leap and sat down on each side of him, and they looked savagely at him with their fiery eyes.

After a short time, when they had warmed themselves, they said: "Comrade, shall we have a game of cards?" "Why not?" he replied, "but just show me your paws." Then they stretched out their claws. "Oh," said he, "what long nails you have! Wait, I must first cut them for you." Thereupon he seized them by the throats, put them on the cutting board and screwed their feet fast. "I have looked at your fingers," said he, "and my fancy for card playing has gone," and he struck them dead and threw them out into the water.

But when he had done away with these two, and was about to sit down again by his fire, out from every hole and corner came black cats with red-hot eyes, and more and more of them came until he could no longer move, and they yelled horribly, and got on his fire, pulled it to pieces, and tried to put it out. He watched them for a while quietly, but at last when they were going too far, he seized his cutting knife and cried, "Away with you, vermin," and began to cut them down. Some of them ran away; the others he killed and threw out into the fish pond.

When he came back, he fanned the embers of his fire again and warmed himself. And as he thus sat, his eyes would keep open no longer, and he felt a desire to sleep. Then he looked round and saw a great bed in the corner. "That is the very thing for me," said he, and got into it. When he was just going to shut his eyes, however, the bed began to move of its own accord, and went over the

whole of the castle. "That's right," he said, "but go faster." Then the bed rolled on as if six horses were harnessed to it, up and down, over thresholds and stairs, but suddenly hop, hop, it turned over upside down, and lay on him like a mountain. But he threw quilts and pillows up in the air, got out, and said, "Now anyone who likes may drive," and lay down by his fire, and slept till it was day.

In the morning the King came, and when he saw him lying there on the ground, he thought the evil spirits had killed him. Then he said, "After all it is a pity for so hand-some a man." The youth heard it, got up, and said, "It has not come to that yet." Then the King was astonished, but very glad, and asked how he had fared. "Very well indeed," answered he, "one night is past, the two oth-ers will pass likewise." Then he went to the innkeeper, who opened his eyes very wide, and said: "I never expected to see you alive again! Have you learned how to shudder yet?" "No," said he, "it is all in vain. If someone would but tell me!"

The second night he again went up into the old castle, sat down by the fire, and once more began his old song: "If I could but shudder!" When midnight came, an uproar and noise of tumbling about was heard; at first it was low, but it grew louder and louder. Then it was quiet for a while, but at length, with a loud scream, half a man came down the chimney and fell before him. "Hullo!" cried he, "another half belongs to this. This is not enough!" Then the uproar began again, there was a roaring and howling, and the other half fell down likewise.

"Wait," said he, "I will just stoke up the fire a little for you." When he had done that and looked round again, the two pieces had joined together and a hideous man was sitting in his place. "That is no part of our bargain," said the youth, "the bench is mine." The man wanted to push him away; the youth, however, would not allow that, but thrust him off with all his strength, and seated himself again in his own place.

Then still more men fell down the chimney, one after the other; they brought nine dead men's legs and two skulls, and set them up and played at nine-pins with them. The youth also wanted to play and said: "Listen you, can I join you?" "Yes, if you have any money." "Money enough," replied he, "but your balls are not quite round." Then he took the skulls and put them in the lathe and turned them till they were. "There, now they will roll better!" said he. "Hurrah! Now we'll have fun!" He played with them and lost some of his money, but when the clock struck twelve, everything vanished from his sight. He lay down and quietly fell asleep.

Next morning the King came to inquire after him. "How has it fared with you this time?" asked he. "I have been playing at nine-pins," he answered, "and have lost a couple of farthings." "Have you not shuddered then?" "What?" said he, "I did so that I had fun! If I did but know what it was to shudder!"

The third night he sat down again on his bench and said quite sadly: "If I could but know what it was to shudder." When it grew late, six tall men came in and brought a coffin. Then said he, "Ha, ha! That is certainly my little cousin who died only a few days ago," and he beckoned with his finger, and cried: "Come, little cousin, come." The tall men placed the coffin on the ground, but he went to it and took the lid off, and a dead man lay therein. He felt his face, but it was cold as ice. "Wait," said he, "I will warm you a little," and went to the fire and warmed his hand and laid it on the dead man's face, but he remained cold. Then he took the body out, sat down by the fire, laid him on his lap, and rubbed his arms so that the blood might

circulate again. As this also did no good, he thought to himself, "When two people lie in bed together, they warm each other," and carried him to the bed, covered him over, and lay down by him. After a short time the dead man became warm, too, and began to move. Then said the youth, "See, little cousin, have I not warmed you!" The dead man, however, got up and cried: "Now will I strangle you."

"What!" said he, "is that the way you thank me? You shall at once go into your coffin again," and he took him up, threw him into it, and shut the lid. Then came the six men, and carried him away again. "I cannot manage to shudder," said he. "I shall never learn it here as long as I live."

Then a man entered who was taller than all the others and looked terrible. He was old, however, and had a long white beard. "You wretch," cried he, "you shall soon learn what it is to shudder, for you shall die." "Not so fast," replied the youth. "If I am to die, I shall have to have a say in it." "I will soon seize you," said the fiend. "Softly, softly, do not act so big. I am as strong as you are, and perhaps even stronger." "We shall see," said the old man. "If you are stronger, I will let you go—come, we will try."

Then he led him by dark passages to a smith's forge, took an ax, and with one blow, struck an anvil into the ground. "I can do better than that," said the youth, and went to the other anvil. The old man placed himself near, wanting to look on, and his white beard hung down. Then the youth seized the ax, split the anvil with one blow, and in it caught the old man's beard. "Now I have you," said the youth. "Now it is your turn to die."

Then he seized an iron bar and beat the old man until he moaned and entreated him to stop, when he would give him great riches. The youth drew out the ax and let him go. The old man led him back into the castle, and in a cellar showed him three chests of gold. "Of these," said he, "one part is for the poor, the other for the King, the third is yours." In the meantime the clock struck twelve, and the spirit disappeared, so that the youth stood in darkness. "I shall still be able to find my way out," said he, and felt about, found the way into the room, and fell asleep there by his fire.

Next morning the King came and said: "Now you must have learned what shuddering is!" "No," he answered, "what can it be? My dead cousin was here, and a bearded man came and showed me a great deal of money down below, but no one told me what it was to shudder."

"Then," said the King, "you have released the castle, and shall marry my daughter." "That is all very well," said he, "but still I do not know what it is to shudder!"

The gold was brought up and the wedding celebrated; but howsoever much the young King loved his wife, and however cheerful he was, he still said always: "If I could but shudder—if I could but shudder." And this at last angered her. Her waiting maid said: "I will find a cure for him; he shall soon learn what it is to shudder."

She went out to the stream that flowed through the garden and had a whole bucketful of gudgeons brought to her.

At night when the young King was sleeping, his wife was to draw the covers off him and empty the bucketful of cold water with the gudgeons in it over him, so that the little fishes would sprawl about him. Then he woke up and cried: "Oh, what makes me shudder so?—What makes me shudder so, dear wife? Ah! Now I know what it is to shudder—at last I know what it is to shudder!"

TRACY ARAH DOCKRAY

Tracy Arah Dockray mastered sculpture at Pratt Institute. Recognizing a long-time interest in children's books, she began to work with Play-Doh® as her medium. As a result, she produced a four-book series, the first of which is *My Play-Doh Book of Animals* (Playskool Books, an imprint of Dutton Children's Books/Penguin USA, 1996). She has illustrated *Microaliens,* by Howard Tomb and Dennis Kunkel (Farrar Straus Giroux, 1994) and *Delia at the Delano,* a book written by Bob Morris and privately published in 1996 by Ian Schrager. A self-taught painter, she is now living happily ever after in New York City with her tiny spotted dog, Zeus.

MARIA TATAR

Maria Tatar teaches folklore, children's literature, and cultural studies at Harvard University. She is the author of *The Hard Facts of the Grimms' Fairy Tales* (1978) and *Off With Their Heads! Fairy Tales and the Culture of Childhood* (1987), as well as *Spellbound: Studies on Mesmerism and Literature* (1978) and *Lustmord: Sexual Murder in Weimar Germany* (1995), all published by Princeton University Press. Ms. Tatar is currently at work on a study of literary and folkloric inflections of the Bluebeard story and on an anthology of fairy tales to be published with W. W. Norton & Co. She lives in Cambridge, Massachusetts, with her two children.